'I know what you want, Nik!' Her eyes flashed deeply purple in the illumination of the street lamp, her tiny hands clenched into fists at her sides.

'You want to make a film of *No Ordinary Boy*. In the hopes, no doubt, of adding yet another Oscar to the five you already have in your trophy cabinet!'

God, this woman was beautiful when roused, whether to anger or passion. And at this moment Nik knew exactly which one he wanted it to be!

'Perhaps I should feel flattered that you know I have five Oscars—'

'And perhaps you shouldn't!'

'Another Oscar would be nice,' he conceded huskily. 'But at this moment I'm damned if I wouldn't settle for a night in bed with you!'

THE PRINCE BROTHERS

Enter the glamorous world of these gorgeous men...

Enter the glamorous world of the movies when you read
about the love lives of the celebrity Prince brothers,
owners of the prestigious company PrinceMovies.

Each brother is super-successful in his field:

Arrogant, forceful and determined, the oldest,
Nik, is a movie director.
Enjoy his story in

PRINCE'S PASSION
October 2005

A former bad boy, **Zak** is now a world-famous actor,
known for being a charming rogue.
Meet him in

PRINCE'S PLEASURE
November 2005

And the youngest, **Rik,** is a screenwriter who's more
reserved than his brothers, but very charming.
You can read about his life in

PRINCE'S LOVE-CHILD
January 2006

PRINCE'S PASSION

BY
CAROLE MORTIMER

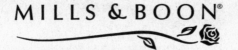
MILLS & BOON®

For Peter, as always.

First published in Great Britain 2005
Harlequin Mills & Boon Limited,
Eton House, 18-24 Paradise Road, Richmond, Surrey TW9 1SR

© Carole Mortimer 2005

ISBN 0 263 84188 X

Set in Times Roman 10½ on 12 pt.
01-1005-47249

Printed and bound in Spain
by Litografía Rosés, S.A., Barcelona

PROLOGUE

'SO WHAT did your elusive author have to say to my offer this time?' Nik prompted the publisher as the two men faced each other across the other man's desk, his American accent muted with deceptive boredom.

Deceptive, because Nik was anything but bored when it came to acquiring the movie rights to J. I. Watson's emotive book...

James Stephens looked uncomfortable. A man in his mid-fifties, head of Stephens Publishing since his father had retired over twenty years ago, James had obviously seen it all when it came to the often unpredictable temperaments of the authors who wrote for him.

But Nik's assessing gaze beneath lowered lids could see that the other man was as baffled by the attitude of the author J. I. Watson as Nik was himself.

What was so difficult about him wanting to acquire the movie rights to the book that had taken the publishing world by storm six months ago? Surely it was every author's dream to have their book turned into a movie? A movie—and even if Nik did say this himself!—to be produced and directed by none other than the Oscar-winning Nikolas Prince?

But no, of the four letters sent to the author in the last two months, the first two had gone unanswered, the third one had resulted in a polite but terse refusal of the proposal, and Nik had yet to hear a response after the fourth. But from the resigned look on James Stephens's face, it was yet another refusal.

To be truthful, Nik had found the last two months of waiting to meet J. I. Watson increasingly frustrating. A month ago he had even wined and dined the female senior editor here who dealt with the author in the hopes that he could bypass James Stephens altogether and get straight to the author himself. After several dinners Jane Morrow had become relaxed enough in his company to confide in him, after making him promise not to reveal his source, that the author's real name was Nixon. But she had gone on to admit that this little nugget of information wouldn't be too much of a help to him, because the publishers always corresponded with the author through a PO box.

'He turned my offer down again,' Nik guessed grimly now.

'Yes,' James confirmed, obviously relieved not to have to say the words himself.

'What's wrong with the man?' Nik stood up forcefully, a big man, well over six feet tall, his dark hair overlong and slightly unkempt, glittering grey eyes dominating his hard-hewn features. 'Does he want more money? Is that it?' he speculated. 'I'll give him whatever he wants. Within reason.'

James sighed, a slightly built man with receding brown hair, only the shrewd light in his blue eyes to belie his otherwise amiable appearance. 'Perhaps if I show you the latest letter we've received…?' He opened a file on his desk, picking up the top sheet of paper to hand it to Nik.

There was only a single line printed on the paper: 'Not even if Nik Prince were to ask me himself!'

Succinct. To the point. An unmistakable refusal.

And yet, irritating as it certainly was, it wasn't that one-line refusal that caught and held Nik's attention as he continued to look at the letter. For printed at the top of the letter was the PO box number Jane had mentioned, and it was right here in London, of all places. A fact that James Stephens had probably forgotten when he'd offered to let Nik look at the letter...

Nik looked up at the publisher, silver gaze narrowed as he handed back the letter without comment; he had no doubts that James Stephens was an honourable man, that if he realized he had breached his author's anonymity by letting Nik see the place of the PO box, he would most likely contact the man immediately and get him to change their point of contact.

'Have you tried talking to the man face to face—no?' He frowned as James shook his head.

James sighed heavily. 'I've never met him—'

'Never?' Nik echoed incredulously; this was turning into something of a farce. James had stonewalled him from the beginning concerning meeting J. I. Watson, but Nik couldn't have guessed that that was because the other man had never met the author, either!

The publisher grimaced. 'Never met him. Never seen him. Never spoken to him,' he rasped. 'No telephone number ever supplied, you see. In fact, our contact has only ever been through the mail.'

'I don't believe this!' Nik dropped back down into the chair facing the desk, totally bemused by what he had just learnt. Thanks to Jane Morrow he knew about the PO box, but he had thought that point of contact had been set up after meetings between the author and publisher. 'All this time I've assumed this reclusive thing was just a publishers' publicity stunt!'

'I wish!' James muttered frustratedly. 'But the truth is we received the unsolicited manuscript almost eighteen months ago. A junior editor eventually read it, quickly passing it on to a more senior colleague once she realized

the quality of writing and storyline. The manuscript finally arrived on the senior editor's desk after being in-
house for almost three months—that's actually not bad!'
he defended as Nik gave him a scathing glance.

'If you say so,' Nik murmured, still stunned by the
knowledge that no one at this prestigious publishing
house had ever met the author who had made millions
for them, as well as for himself, over the last six months.

Jane Morrow certainly hadn't chosen to confide *that*
important snippet of information to him!

'I do say so.' James sat up straighter in his high-backed
leather chair. 'We have, of course, asked to meet Mr
Watson on several occasions, but all to no avail,' he continued firmly as Nik would have made another scathing
comment. 'Every approach has been met with a firm refusal.'

Nik shook his head. No wonder he was having such
difficulty trying to do a deal with the author if the man
refused to even meet with his own publishing house!

'It's true,' James Stephens assured him, obviously mis-
understanding the reason for the shake of Nik's head.
'The contract, editorial suggestions—although I have to
admit there weren't too many of those,' he acknowledged
admiringly. 'Everything was done through the post.'

'But what do you do about fan mail, things like that?
Do you send all that off through the mail, too?' Nik
asked.

James shook his head, pulling another file on his desk
towards him, a file filled to overflowing. 'We send him
a selection every now and then, just so that he knows
how his public feels about the book. But none of the
nastier ones, of course; those are all dealt with in-house.'

'Nastier ones?' Nik raised an eyebrow.

'The insulting ones.' James shrugged. 'Death threats,'

he clarified. 'This much overnight success tends to bring out the worst in some people.'

Oh, Nik could believe that; he had received more than his own fair share of nasty letters over the years. 'The contract.' He picked up on the one point in James's earlier statement that might have relevance to his own needs. 'Surely—'

'The clause concerning film and television rights was taken out,' James cut in as he easily guessed Nik's next question. 'At the author's request, of course.' Blue eyes twinkled merrily.

'Of course.' Nik scowled; why shouldn't the other man's eyes glitter with laugher—after all, Stephens Publishing was already laughing all the way to the bank!

James grinned unrepentantly. 'We wanted the book, under any terms we could get it.'

Nik felt sure that a book like *No Ordinary Boy* only came along once in a publishing lifetime, so he couldn't blame the other man for grabbing the manuscript, regardless of any terms the author cared to make. If he hadn't, then another publishing house certainly would have done.

Not that any of that was of help to Nik now; he wanted to make a movie of the book, and without the author's cooperation there was no way he was going to be able to do that.

'You think *you* feel frustrated?' James shook his head. 'Can you imagine the mileage we've lost by not being able to produce the author, to provide personal interviews, book signings, things like that? Watson's reclusive attitude has probably lost us millions in sales.'

'But you've made millions, anyway,' Nik drawled knowingly. 'And I don't suppose my acquiring the movie rights would do you any harm, either.'

'No,' the other man acknowledged with a smile. 'But as you *aren't* going to acquire the movie rights—'

'Who says I'm not?' Nik cut in ruthlessly, his expression once again grim as he stood up.

James looked up at him curiously. 'What makes you think *you'll* be successful in meeting and talking to the man when we've been trying for months to no avail?'

'That's easy.' Nik smiled confidently. 'I don't play by the same rules as you do, James.' And now that he had the PO box number, and its point of origin, he had every intention of pursuing J. I. Watson—or should he say Nixon?—in any way open to him. 'Watson's claim ''not even if Nik Prince were to ask me himself'' is shortly going to become fact,' he assured James grimly. 'And, I should warn you, I never take no for an answer!' Nik added harshly.

Neither did he intend doing so this time. As J. I. Watson was shortly going to find out!

CHAPTER ONE

'THANKS for inviting me, Susan.' Jinx smiled brightly at the other woman as she opened the door to her, the sound of a party audible in the background.

The two women had been at school together, and Susan was now married to a partner of an accountancy firm, their two small children safely asleep upstairs. Or, if they weren't, the live-in nanny would make sure they didn't interrupt the party being given to celebrate their parents' fifth wedding anniversary.

Susan gave a disbelieving snort. 'Don't give me that, Jinx; you and I both know you would much rather be at home with a good book, that I had to practically twist your arm at lunch earlier this week to get you to agree to come tonight! But thanks, anyway; it simply wouldn't have been the same without the presence of our one and only bridesmaid.' She moved to kiss Jinx warmly on the cheek before standing back and looking at her frowningly. Jinx was small and slender, the black dress she wore perfect with her long, flowing, fiery red hair. 'Tell me, how is it that you seem to get younger every year and I just get more matronly?'

'Flatterer,' Jinx scoffed, handing her friend the peach-coloured roses she had brought with her as a present; the same colour roses that had adorned Susan's bouquet at her wedding five years ago.

'Oh, Jinx, they're beautiful!' Susan beamed. 'But tell me, how's Jack?'

Jinx's smile didn't falter, although her eyes shadowed

a little. 'About the same.' She shrugged. 'But where's your handsome husband?' she prompted mischievously, deciding the subject of her father was something better not discussed at her friend's celebration party.

'Here I am,' Leo announced happily, moving past Susan to easily sweep the diminutive Jinx up into his arms and kiss her firmly on her lips. 'It's still not too late for us to run away together, you know,' he told her *sotto voce*, blue eyes twinkling merrily as he received a playful punch on the arm from his grinning wife.

'Sounds like a good party.' Jinx nodded in the direction of Susan and Leo's drawing-room where the sound of chatter and laughter, the chinking of glasses, could easily be heard.

'We have a surprise guest,' her friend told her excitedly as she linked her arm with Jinx's to walk down the plushly carpeted hallway in the direction of the noisy enjoyment. 'You know we had Stazy Hunter design our drawing-room last year?' she prompted as Jinx did her best to look interested; as Susan knew only too well this sort of scene really wasn't her idea of fun.

As the decoration of the now-beautiful gold and terracotta room had been Susan's main topic of conversation six months ago, of course Jinx was aware that the famous Stazy Hunter had been the designer.

Susan nodded, not really requiring an answer. 'Well, we've stayed friends, so of course I invited Stazy, and her husband Jordan, to join us this evening, and then an hour ago Stazy telephoned to ask if she could possibly bring her brother with her as he had arrived unexpectedly, and of course I said yes, and you'll never guess who Stazy's brother turned out to be—'

'She'll pause for breath in a minute,' Leo reassured Jinx dryly as he fell into step beside them, draping his arm affectionately across his wife's shoulders. 'But you know Jinx isn't interested in that sort of thing, Susan. Now if this chap were a university professor or an archaeologist, something like that, then she might be more interested, but as he's only a—'

'Leo is only being so negative because the man's gorgeous,' Susan huffed. 'Absolutely gorgeous,' she repeated enthusiastically. 'Six foot three of pure sexual magnetism—'

'And what am I?' Leo interrupted.

'Oh, you're gorgeous too, darling,' Susan assured him distractedly.

'Just not as gorgeous—or sexually magnetic!—as our esteemed guest,' he acknowledged ruefully.

'Well…I'm married to you.' Susan pouted. 'It isn't the same.'

'No, I can see that it isn't.' Leo grimaced. 'Are you sure you wouldn't like to run away with me, Jinx?'

Jinx gave the expected dismissive laugh. 'You know as well as I do that you love Susan to distraction!'

Leo shook his head. 'That could change if she's going to go around enthusing about famous film directors!'

Jinx's eyes widened in alarm. 'Stazy Hunter's brother is a film director?'

'Yes, he's—sorry.' Susan gave a rueful smile as the doorbell rang again. 'Catch up with you later.' She squeezed Jinx's arms before grabbing her husband's hand and dragging him off to answer the door with her.

Jinx turned to enter the drawing-room—and instantly found herself face to face with what she was pretty sure was Susan's 'six foot three of pure sexual magnetism'!

Well…not exactly face to face—she was only five feet one inch in her stockinged feet, the two-inch heels on her shoes still making her a foot shorter than the man who returned her gaze with compelling silver-grey eyes, his mouth hard and unsmiling.

A man she easily recognized as Nik Prince. One-time actor, now an extremely successful film director, the eldest of the three brothers who owned PrinceMovies, one of America's most prestigious film companies.

A shutter came down over her eyes of violet-blue, that curious shade between blue and purple, her pointed chin rising challengingly as Nik Prince looked down at her with an assessment that was totally male. And for that brief moment, a mere matter of seconds, it was as if the two of them were the only people in the room, the noisy chatter, the laughter, the background music all fading away as steely silver-grey clashed with violet-blue.

Jinx became very conscious of the flowing red hair down her back, the perfect fit of her knee-length black dress above long, silky legs. But most of all the man's size, the sheer animal magnetism emanating from him despite the civilized attire of black evening suit and snowy white shirt, made her aware of each nerve and pulse in her own body, every part of her seeming to tingle with awareness, her breasts rising pert and aroused beneath the silky material of her dress.

As if drawn by a magnet, that intent grey gaze dropped down to the level of her breasts, lingering, as tangible as any caress, as if the man had reached out and physically touched her there.

But it was the amusement that glimmered in those hard grey eyes, the knowing smile that curved the perfect symmetry of that cynical mouth, as if completely aware of the effect he was having on her—and why shouldn't he be? This man was almost forty years old, obviously experienced, his affairs over the years with his leading ladies legendary! That was what enabled Jinx to break the force of his gaze, her own mouth curving derisively now.

'Well?' she challenged him.

Dark brows rose. 'Well, what?' The voice was low and husky, the American drawl giving it a sexy quality that made a nonsense of the actual words he said—his tone said 'let's go to bed', so sensual was its inflexion.

Jinx's direct gaze didn't falter for a second. 'Do you like what you see?'

He smiled fully now, showing even white teeth, lines etched beside his eyes and mouth. 'Wouldn't any man?' he taunted her.

'I wasn't asking "any man",' Jinx snapped. 'I was asking *you*.'

Nik Prince took a step towards her, bringing him dangerously close, so close she could feel the heat from his body, smell the tangy aroma of his aftershave. 'Yes, I like what I see,' he murmured huskily. 'But, then, you already knew that,' he added. 'How would you feel about the two of us making our excuses and getting out of here?'

Jinx blinked, the only sign she gave—she hoped!— that she was stunned by his suggestion. It would be surprising coming from any man on such short acquaintance, but Nik Prince was no ordinary man!

She usually made a point of avoiding parties like this one, had only made the effort to come this evening because she was so fond of Susan and Leo. But if Nik Prince thought she was the sort of party girl who allowed herself to be picked up by men like him, then he was in for a disappointment.

'Wouldn't that be rather rude to Susan and Leo?' she retorted critically.

'Are they our host and hostess?' he asked with an un-

interested glance in their direction as they stood further
down the hallway greeting yet more guests. 'I don't know
them and they don't know me; why should it bother me
what they think?'

Why, indeed? In fact, from what she had heard of this
man, he tended to be a law unto himself, was reputed to
be an uncompromising film director, an inflexible head
of his family of two younger brothers and a sister, his
relationships with women, be they beautiful actresses or
otherwise, always short-lived.

In fact, he wasn't Jinx's type at all. If she had a type.
It had been so long since there had been anyone in her
life in a romantic way that she had forgotten!

She gave a shrug of slender shoulders. 'Because they
were gracious enough to extend their hospitality to you
on very short notice might be one way of looking at it,
don't you think?' she rebuked.

He gave a mocking inclination of his head. 'I stand
corrected,' he drawled, grey eyes warm as he smiled
down at her.

That genuine smile, when it came, was well worth
waiting for. In fact, Jinx felt slightly breathless and not
a little shaky at the knees. Not a very sensible response
given the circumstances!

'Good,' she bit out with more force than she had intended, deliberately turning away from him as she took
a step back, once again widening the distance between
them. 'Now, if you will excuse me, Mr Prince—' She
broke off abruptly as he reached out a hand to lightly
grasp her arm, his fingers long and strong, their warmth
seeming to penetrate her silky skin.

'You obviously know my name, but I don't know
yours,' he said huskily as she looked up at him enquiringly.

Jinx felt shaken by the effect of his touch, a surge like electricity having coursed through her. Her breathing suddenly became shallow and uneven, and her eyes widened with surprise at her own response.

Nik Prince tilted his head to one side. 'Let's see... You don't look like a Joan. Or a Cynthia. Or a—'

'Tell me, does this chat-up line usually work?' Jinx cut in, having finally come to her senses enough to know that this man was dangerous—with a capital D!

Nik Prince didn't look too put out by her mockery; in fact, he was standing far too close again, those grey eyes gleaming with laughter. 'Believe it or not, I don't usually need a chat-up line.'

Oh, she believed it, all right. She was sure this man usually had women lining up to be with him rather than his having to pursue them. 'Perhaps that's as well,' she told him dryly.

Grey eyes warmed as he smiled his appreciation of her deliberate put-down. 'You'll have to excuse me; it's been a while,' he conceded wryly.

Jinx wasn't in the least interested in how long it had been. 'If you wouldn't mind releasing my arm...?' she prompted, having made several unsuccessful attempts to do so herself.

'But I do mind,' he murmured throatily, his thumb moving in a rhythmic caress against her inner wrist now.

'But so do I,' she snapped. 'Now, if you'll excuse me...? I must just go over and say hello to Susan's parents.' Thank goodness she had just spotted their familiar faces across the room.

Nik Prince moved his hand, but only to take a proprietorial hold of her elbow instead. 'How about you introduce me? I can say hello to them too, and then I'll finally know your name.'

She met his gaze unblinkingly. 'My name is Juliet.'

His eyes widened momentarily, as if that wasn't quite what he had expected to hear—as, indeed, it probably wasn't!—and then his considerable acting skills took over and he gave an acknowledging inclination of his head. 'Now that's more like it.'

'That hardly makes you my Romeo, Mr Prince.'

'Pity,' he drawled. 'And it's Nik.'

'Nik,' she accepted shortly.

'Okay.' He smiled his satisfaction with her compliance. 'And what do you do, Juliet?'

'Do?' she delayed warily.

'Careerwise. Or have I committed some sort of social gaffe and you don't do anything?'

The amusement in his tone annoyed her intensely. 'What I do, Mr—Nik,' she corrected irritably as he gave her a reproving look, 'is teach. History. At Cambridge University.' She tried to keep that slight tone of pride out of her voice when she said the latter, knowing she had failed miserably as his firmly sculptured mouth twisted mockingly. 'Although I'm in the middle of taking a year's sabbatical at the moment,' she enlarged.

'And does that make you a Dr Something?'

'It does. Now if you will excuse me? I know I may have arrived on my own this evening, but that really doesn't mean that I am on my own,' she pointed out.

'Well, of course you aren't—I'm here now.'

Jinx gave him an exasperated frown. 'That isn't what I meant and you know it!'

'Do I?'

'Yes,' she easily dismissed his too-innocent expression.

'I see.' He glanced around the room. 'And which one

of the twenty or so men here tonight is going to come over and claim you?'

Jinx felt the colour warm her cheeks. No one was going to 'come over and claim her', because at twenty-eight she was single, had never been married, and probably never would be.

She straightened her shoulders, at the same time shrugging off his hand under her elbow. 'I really don't think that is any of your concern, Mr Prince,' she told him quietly, stepping completely away from him now as she turned and walked across the room.

But she was totally aware, with every step that she took, that Nik Prince was watching the sensuous sway of her hips!

Nik stood and watched the redhead's departure with narrowed, enigmatic eyes.

Damn. He hadn't made too good a job of that, now had he? He really must be rusty when it came to the art of seduction. Because Juliet 'Jinx' Nixon certainly hadn't been seduced!

He'd had to wait days for the man he had hired to watch the post office box to confirm that a girl came to collect the mail at twelve-thirty every day. Nik had then taken over himself, only to realize, on closer inspection, when she had arrived, that she wasn't a girl at all, just a very petite woman. The denims, tee shirt and baseball cap she'd worn had served to disguise her age. Deliberately so? He had thought so.

In fact he'd been totally convinced of it when she'd gone outside to the adjacent car park, unlocked a Volkswagen Golf, and thrown her mail in the back of the car before removing the baseball cap and shaking out the long length of her fiery red hair. Then she'd thrown the cap in the back with her letters before taking out a tailored jacket and pulling it on over the tee shirt.

The transformation from a teenager like almost every other teenager Nik had been able to see walking down the street, to a beautifully elegant older woman, had taken only a little adjustment of the clothing and an application of a deep peach lipgloss.

Nik had followed her as she'd taken a shoulder bag from the back of the car and set off down the street, standing well back when she'd gone into a busy Italian bistro and met a beautiful blonde woman for lunch. Susan Fellows, he had learnt afterwards after quizzing one of the busy waitresses. When, incidentally, his seductive tone had been more than successful!

A couple of conversations with his sister Stazy later— a young lady residing in London herself with her husband and baby son, and more intimately acquainted with the London social scene than he was—and he'd known exactly who Susan Fellows was. Even more interesting than that, he had quickly discovered that her luncheon companion was a very good friend of Susan's called Jinx Nixon.

It hadn't taken too many more enquiries to learn that Jinx's father was Jackson Ivor Nixon, also a university professor who taught history, and an authority on the Jacobite uprisings, author of several prestigious books on the subject. Nik had put two and two together and realized that Jackson Ivor Nixon also had to be J. I. Watson, the author of *No Ordinary Boy*…

Nik had also figured out why he preferred to remain anonymous; Jackson I. Nixon was an extremely well-respected author of several historical tomes. *No Ordinary Boy*, while being a runaway success, was actually a book written for children, but which had been taken up and read by adults and children alike, about a young boy of twelve confined to a wheelchair who suddenly became a superhero. Not exactly Jackson I. Nixon material!

And following Jinx, having her checked out, wasn't the most scrupulously honest thing he had ever done, Nik allowed ruefully, but a necessary evil as far as he was concerned. As had been the seduction scene when Jinx had arrived at her friend's party a few minutes ago.

Not that it had been too much of a hardship; Juliet 'Jinx' Nixon was an extremely beautiful woman.

She hadn't seemed too impressed with him, though! Nik winced inwardly. Never mind, it was early days yet. He wasn't known for his patience when it came to directing temperamental actors and actresses, but when it came to something he wanted, then he could be extremely patient, indeed. And he wanted the movie rights to J. I. Watson's book. Jinx Nixon's father's book...

'Exactly what are you up to, big brother of mine?' Stazy linked her arm through his as she looked up at him knowingly. 'And don't say nothing,' she warned mischievously. 'I know you far too well for that. And I saw you make a beeline for that beautiful redhead the moment she came in the door.'

He never had been able to put too much over on Stazy. At twenty-two she was seventeen years his junior, and had been the single constant weakness in his life from the moment she was born. Her marriage to Jordan Hunter just over a year ago, and the birth of her son Sam three months ago, had given her a confidence that brooked no refusal.

'In fact,' Stazy continued thoughtfully, a beautiful redhead herself, although at five feet nine inches tall she would completely dwarf the petite Jinx Nixon, 'now that

I think about it, it was almost as if you were waiting for her to arrive. Nik, what—?'

'Don't worry about it, honey,' he advised with a pat on the hand she rested on his arm.

'But I do worry about it, Nik,' she persisted.

He gave a resigned sigh. When Stazy got her teeth into something, she was apt not to let go. Since her successful marriage to Jordan she had been more than a little obvious in her marriage-making plans for her three older brothers. And as all three of the Prince brothers were in England at the moment in preparation for baby Sam's christening tomorrow, she was taking full advantage of this opportunity to play matchmaker...!

'I shouldn't,' he murmured softly, his gaze warning her off the subject.

'No?' She arched auburn brows.

'No,' he confirmed firmly.

The last thing he wanted was for Stazy to take an interest in Jinx Nixon; he already had his work cut out trying to maneouvre a meeting with the other woman's father, without contending with Stazy's machinations, too!

'Okay,' his sister capitulated. 'In that case, come over and say hello to some of the other guests.'

Nik eyed her warily for several seconds, not in the least fooled by her easy acquiescence. But other than pursuing the subject himself, something he had no intention of doing, there was nothing else he could say or do to put his mind at rest.

However, he did keep a close eye on Jinx Nixon's movements over the next hour or so. He noted with satisfaction, despite what she had said earlier, that she didn't spend more than a few minutes in any other man's company—while at the same time totally avoiding his!

'Can I drive you home?'

Jinx turned and frowned at Nik when he spoke to her. He'd stood and watched her as she'd slowly edged her way over to the door, seeming on the verge of making her excuses to leave. 'I beg your pardon?'

Nik moved to stand in front of her, effectively blocking out the rest of the room, leaving the two of them co-cooned in a bubble of intimacy. 'I asked if I could drive you home,' he repeated mildly—of course, that was on the assumption that Jordan wouldn't mind getting a cab home for himself and Stazy and letting Nik borrow his car for a couple of hours!

Jinx shook her head, her hair gleaming copper-red in the candlelight that illuminated the room. 'I have my own car. Thank you,' she added belatedly.

He nodded. 'Which you aren't going to drive.'

'I'm not?' Her eyes had widened, deep blue eyes that could appear almost purple in some lights.

In this light, Nik noticed appreciatively. Also her skin was that pale peach of most redheads, smooth and clear, a tiny pulse beating at the base of her throat. A throat he ached to kiss, he suddenly realized.

'No,' he confirmed huskily. 'You've drunk two glasses of wine, which means you're already over the limit—'

'You've been counting?' she interrupted incredulously, angry colour heightening in her cheeks.

'Don't worry about it.' He shrugged. 'I have that sort of mind. For instance, the man standing beside the fire-place has so far drunk a whole bottle of champagne to himself and is now about to start on another. The brunette at his side is obviously the driver for the evening, has only had three glasses of orange juice, and is obviously very pi—annoyed about it,' he corrected wryly. 'The man near the window—'

'Okay, I get the picture,' Jinx snapped. 'But even so...'

'Even so...?' Nik prompted softly.

She looked resentful. 'I'm not sure I like the idea of having someone watching me that closely.'

'The only way you can stop that is to not be quite so watchable—which, with your face and body, just isn't going to happen,' Nik teased her.

She gave him a perplexed frown, obviously not quite sure how to take that last remark, whether to be flattered or insulted by it. In the end, it seemed, she decided to ignore it. 'Nevertheless, I won't be requiring your offer of a lift home,' she dismissed with obvious relief.

Not very flattering to his ego, Nik acknowledged. In fact, Jinx Nixon's attitude towards him hadn't exactly been warm all evening. His only consolation was that she hadn't been warm towards any other man, either!

Apart from perhaps Leo Fellows, their host, Nik corrected himself with an inward frown. The two of them had seemed to be enjoying a flirtatious conversation half an hour or so ago. Could it possibly be that the reason Jinx had arrived here alone this evening was because she was involved in an affair with her best friend's husband? It wouldn't be the first time—in fact it was all too common.

Nik found the thought more than slightly unpleasant when made in connection with the beautiful Jinx Nixon—and no matter what she might have told him her name was, he knew that her closest friends called her Jinx.

And that was his plan, wasn't it? To get close to Jinx, wheedle an introduction to her father, and present him with the contract for movie rights to *No Ordinary Boy*.

What could be simpler?

Well, Jinx Nixon being a little less beautiful and a whole lot less sexy would have been a help!

He had expected to engage in a little light seduction—it was a dirty job, but someone had to do it!—but finding Jinx Nixon so attractive, his senses roused just inhaling her perfume, and other parts of him roused every time he so much as looked at her, had definitely not been part of that plan...

CHAPTER TWO

'Why not?'

Jinx smiled confidently in the face of Nik Prince's obvious displeasure at having her turn down his offer of a lift home. 'Susan's parents live only half a mile away from me and have already offered to drive me home later.' Although, she had to admit, she had been on the point of forgoing that offer and simply leaving!

She found this man altogether too disturbing, which was why she hadn't looked his way at all since they'd parted earlier, even though she had been conscious of his every move.

In fact, she had never been this aware of a man in her life before. Of course that awareness was on more than one level. On the surface she was aware of the letters received from Stephens Publishing, on this man's behalf, requesting a meeting with the author of *No Ordinary Boy*, in order to discuss acquiring the film rights. But underneath all that she was aware of a physical attraction to Nik Prince that she was trying desperately to ignore.

Obviously, his height and sheer size would dominate any company he was in. The forcefulness of his personality likewise. But it wasn't either of those things that made her skin tingle and heightened her senses just being in the same room with him. No, the attraction she felt towards this man was something she simply couldn't explain, something she had never experienced before.

Or ever wanted to experience again!

'And when you aren't teaching at Cambridge University, home is where?'

Jinx's gaze was guarded as she looked up at Nik. 'London.'

He sighed. 'Which part of London?'

'South west,' she offered unhelpfully, glancing away from the shrewdness in those silver-grey eyes.

As far as she was concerned it was too coincidental, after those letters sent from James Stephens on his behalf, that Nik Prince was here at this party at all. Neither Susan nor Leo had met him before this evening, and he certainly didn't look the type to need his sister to elicit a late invitation, as this one appeared to be, to fill his evening.

No, Jinx had stopped believing in coincidences a long time ago. And Nik Prince being here this evening certainly wasn't one, either. She just wasn't sure how much he knew. But he obviously knew enough—from where, or whom, she wasn't sure—to have arranged to meet her in this roundabout fashion.

But had he been any more prepared than her for the physical awareness that practically sizzled between them?

Somehow she doubted it!

He gave a rueful smile now. 'In other words, you have no intention of telling me where you live?'

'None at all,' she confirmed lightly. That was the very last thing she intended doing!

'Then I had better make the most of my time with you this evening, hadn't I,' he accepted dryly.

Jinx eyed him warily. 'Meaning?'

He gave a shrug of those powerfully broad shoulders. 'There's music in the other room. How about you dance with me as a start?'

A start to what? And did she really want to be that close to him, to feel the heat of his body only inches away from her own, to have him touching her, his hands touching hers, the warmth of his breath against her temple…?

'Scared?' he murmured knowingly.

Jinx straightened immediately, knowing he was goading her in order to achieve his goal, but at the same time unwilling to back down from a man so obviously used to having his own way. 'Not in the least, Mr Prince,' she assured him. 'The truth of the matter is, I can't remember when I last danced; I may have forgotten how.'

'Dancing is like lovemaking,' he told her huskily. 'Once you've tried it, you never forget how!'

So, in spite of her efforts, he was obviously determined to keep this conversation on an intimate level. 'Then I shouldn't have any trouble, should I?' she retorted, turning in the direction of the dining-room where a quartet was softly playing music for the guests to dance to, leaving him to come to his own conclusions concerning her last remark.

She had been right to be apprehensive about allowing this man too close, she acknowledged several minutes later. Nik Prince had ignored all the rules of social etiquette when dancing with a relative stranger, instead pulling her right against him, his arms about her waist, hands linked at the base of her spine, their bodies touching from chest to thigh as they moved slowly to the music.

As far as Jinx was concerned, they might have been the only two people dancing. She was totally aware of Nik as her hands rested on his shoulders, her efforts to maintain a distance between them completely thwarted when Nik reached up and gently laid her head against his shoulder before resting his own head against the silky softness of her hair.

'You smell like flowers,' he murmured close to her ear, his breath as warm as she had known it would be.

'Lily of the Valley soap,' she dismissed pragmatically.

He chuckled softly. 'Are you always this romantic?'

'Are you?' she came back.

'I don't believe it's been one of my character traits to date, no,' he allowed ruefully. 'But that could change,' he added throatily.

This really hadn't been a good idea, Jinx acknowledged with an inward groan. Nik's legs felt hard against her softer ones, the stirring of his thighs unmistakable in such close proximity, the uneven rise and fall of his chest against hers more evidence of his increasing arousal, an arousal that caused a pounding in her own chest and a warmth between her thighs.

'I want you,' Nik groaned, his words accompanied by a gentle nibble against her ear lobe.

Jinx quivered with pleasure, shivers of hot and cold tumbling down her spine. But at the same time she wondered how she could put a stop to this. Because she had to stop it. Now. Before it spiralled out of control.

'There's a woman standing across the room who keeps staring at us,' she told him, hoping to distract him. 'Friend of yours?'

'My sister, Stazy,' Nik answered her without even raising his head, his tongue now tasting the sensitive flesh beneath her ear lobe.

'How can you be sure?' Jinx pursued determinedly, her voice slightly higher than usual as she fought the instinct of her body to curve itself against his, that marauding tongue now seeking the delicate curves of her ear.

Nik chuckled softly, the reverberations only increasing the pleasure of his caresses. 'Stazy has become something of a matchmaker since her own happy marriage a year ago; she's obviously assessing you to see if you're suitable wife material for her eldest—and, may I say, favourite?—brother.'

Jinx pulled back abruptly, staring up at him in disbelief. And then wished she hadn't. He really was the most ruggedly attractive man, and those grey eyes were pure silver now, shining with an intensity of emotion that was unmistakable. Desire. Arousal. For her.

Her own pupils had probably dilated until the black practically obliterated the blue. Revealing desire. Arousal. For him.

She drew in a deep breath. 'In that case, I think it's best that we end this now, don't you?' She stepped back, feeling the momentary tightening of his arms about her before he reluctantly released her, the expression in his eyes one of regret now.

'Why don't we just follow my earlier suggestion and leave here to continue this some place more private?' he asked.

'Like my home?' Jinx challenged.

'Sounds good.' He nodded.

'The home I have no intention of taking you to?' she derided. 'You misunderstood me a few moments ago when I said it's time we end this now, Nik—I meant the charade.'

It was as if a shutter had come down, his eyes no longer silver but a narrowed grey, his expression deliberately—or so it seemed to Jinx—unreadable. 'Charade?' he echoed blandly.

Her mouth twisted humourlessly. 'Look, I know who you are, and you know who I am. I'm not sure how you know—' *yet!* '—but I do know it's totally ridiculous for us to continue with this charade.'

Those grey eyes narrowed even more, several emotions

flickering in their depths, but too briefly for her to analyze.

'Besides,' she added coldly, 'I really see no point in your continuing this seduction act any further.'

'*Act?*' He sounded outraged. 'Do you really think I can just manufacture my attraction to you?'

'I think, Mr Prince, that you are capable of manufacturing anything you feel the inclination to,' she told him candidly, at the same time aware that her attraction to him had been anything but manufactured! 'Now, if you will excuse me, I think my lift is preparing to leave.' She had just spotted Dick and Janet saying their goodnights to the other guests. 'But for the record, Mr Prince,' she paused to add huskily, 'as predicted, having now met you "in person", the answer is still an emphatic *no*! There will be no movie.'

His mouth thinned. 'Isn't that for your father to say, and not you?'

Jinx continued to look at him for several long seconds before giving a slow shake of her head. 'In the circumstances, no, I don't think so,' she answered cautiously.

'What do you mean?' he challenged.

She met his gaze steadily. 'My father isn't a well man, Mr Prince.'

'But all I want is his signature on a piece of paper.'

She gave a humourless smile. 'A signature that would no doubt give you exclusive film rights to *No Ordinary Boy*!'

'Yes,' he bit out, at least sensible enough not to try to deny that was his true interest in pursuing her this evening.

'That isn't going to happen, Mr Prince—'

'Will you call me Nik, damn it?' he cut in harshly. 'In the *circumstances* anything else certainly is ridiculous!'

Jinx didn't need to ask what circumstances he was referring to; their physical response to each other during that dance certainly made a nonsense of any future formality between them.

'Mr Prince. Nik. It's all the same to me.' She gave a dismissive shrug. 'In either case, the answer is still no.'

'As I told James Stephens earlier in the week, I never take no for an answer,' he warned her grimly.

She drew in a sharp breath, unable to hide her surprise at the mention of the publisher. But then how else could Nik have discovered that J. I. Watson's real name was J. I. *Nixon*? 'James Stephens was the one who told you J. I. Watson's real name?'

'James is far too much of a professional to ever do a thing like that,' Nik reproved.

That was something, at least. If Nik Prince's answer had been anything but the one he had just given her then she would have made sure that the second J. I. Watson manuscript, which was even now being prepared for editing, never made it onto James Stephens's desk.

But it was still pretty obvious that someone at Stephens Publishing had to have revealed that confidential information to Nik Prince. The question was, who…?

'Tell me, Mr Prince…' she gave him a considering look '…what is it that you find so difficult to understand about the word no?'

'As far as I can recall, it's not a word that's ever been in my big brother's vocabulary,' a female voice chimed in lightly.

Jinx turned to look at Nik Prince's sister, Stazy Hunter, as she moved to stand next to her brother. The younger woman was extremely beautiful, her red hair almost as bright as Jinx's own. In fact, Stazy Hunter looked a far nicer person altogether than her eldest brother!

'Not at all,' Nik came back smoothly. 'I'm just a positive person rather than a negative one.'

Well, he could be as positive as he wanted as far as Jinx was concerned, because the answer to his request was no, and it would remain no.

'If you'll both excuse me…' She gave Stazy Hunter a vague smile, shot Nik Prince a look of warning, before moving determinedly away from them, inwardly shaken by how close he had got to her.

Too close.

In more ways than one!

Nik frowned frustratedly as he watched Jinx join a middle-aged couple across the room, his gaze narrowing as he considered his two choices of action. One, he could let Jinx just walk out of his life, also taking her knowledge of J. I. Watson with her. Or two, he could make sure that he left with her!

'Do me a favour, will you, Staze?' He turned urgently to his sister.

She looked slightly surprised. 'Of course. If I can. What—'

'Persuade your charming husband that it's time for the two of you to leave.'

Stazy looked nonplussed. 'But it's still early, Nik; what on earth will I tell Susan and Leo—?'

'I don't care what you tell them,' he cut in forcefully, starting to panic slightly as he could see Jinx and the older couple were coming to the end of their goodbyes. 'Your house is on fire. You need to take your husband home and seduce him—'

'Jordan doesn't need any seducing,' Stazy assured him happily.

Nik winced. 'I really didn't need to hear that.' He was

still coming to terms with the fact that his little sister was married at all, let alone to a man as powerful and experienced as Jordan Hunter. 'Okay, find your own excuse, but think of something soon, hmm!'

'Fine.' Stazy held up soothing hands. 'I take it you aren't coming back with us, after all?'

'You take it correct,' he confirmed grimly, his gaze still fixed on Jinx. 'But whatever you're going to do, do it quickly, will you?' Jinx was starting to move towards the door now!

'I'm gone,' his sister assured him—before doing exactly that.

And by the speed with which his sister and brother-in-law made their excuses to their host and hostess, before immediately leaving, Nik had a feeling that the suggestion of seduction might have worked on Jordan, after all!

Nik shook his head. Stazy had made her choice, and it was a choice he wholeheartedly approved of; it was his own problem if he was still having trouble coming to terms with another man being more important to Stazy than he was.

At this moment he had a much more serious situation to deal with!

'Sorry I was delayed.' He hurried to Jinx's side just as she reached the front door, taking a firm hold of her arm before turning to smile warmly at the older couple who accompanied her. 'I hope you don't mind including me in that offer of a lift home?' His tone was deliberately charming. 'My sister was going to drop me at my hotel, but she and Jordan had to get straight back to their house—some sort of emergency...'

The couple shot each other a briefly knowing look before assuring him they didn't mind at all, that there was plenty of room for him in their car.

Not that Nik had thought they would be a problem; it was Jinx's response that could turn this situation around.

He raised questioning brows as he looked down at her, his expression deceptively calm, only the tightening of his fingers on her arm showing evidence of his inner uncertainty as to what her next move would be.

Her eyes were purple as she looked right back at him, anger flaring in their depths, even though she too managed to look outwardly calm.

Come on, Jinx, Nik inwardly encouraged; at least give me a chance.

If he lost sight of her now, then he would have to start all over again tomorrow. Not that he minded doing that, but it would save a hell of a lot of time if she would just be a little more cooperative now.

'Actually—' she turned back to the older couple, smiling '—it really isn't that far. Nik and I can easily walk it.'

'Are you sure, Jinx?' The other woman frowned her uncertainty with the suggestion. 'It's at least a couple of miles,' she explained to Nik.

'But it's such a lovely evening.' Jinx released her arm from Nik's grasp to lightly link it with his. 'I think it would be so much more fun to walk. Don't you, Nik?' she asked sweetly.

Beware the smile of an angry female, he acknowledged ruefully, at the same time happy to fall in with whatever Jinx suggested—as long as it included him. 'Much more fun,' he agreed dryly; a two-mile walk through the Saturday-night revelry of London sounded more like hell to him, but if it ultimately ended up at Jinx's home, the home she shared with her father, then he was willing to put himself through it if she was.

If it ultimately ended up at Jinx's home…

Somehow, after what she had said to him earlier, he had a feeling that wasn't her intention.

'Tell me,' he murmured softly once they had been walking together in silence for some minutes through the balmy streets, Jinx's arm still linked with his own, despite her efforts to release it, 'will we be crossing any bridges on this fun walk home?'

'Several,' she snapped back tautly, obviously not happy with his reluctance to release her.

'That's what I thought.' He grimaced—having a distinct feeling she was considering pushing him over the side of one.

'One thing I can assure you of, Nik,' she bit out tautly. 'I'm not violent.'

'Just private, hmm?' he said knowingly.

'Just private.'

'I've heard several people refer to you as Jinx this evening,' he said in an effort to divert her thoughts.

'Close friends, yes,' she confirmed stiffly—obviously not counting him amongst their number.

Nik disregarded that for the moment; she might not think they were going to be close friends, but he knew better! 'How on earth did you come by such an unusual nickname?'

She shot him a mocking glance. 'Changing the subject?'

'Rapidly,' he confirmed, laughter gleaming in his eyes; the chances of this petitely beautiful woman being able to force his six-foot-three, one-hundred-and-eighty-pound frame over the parapet of a bridge were ludicrous to say the least. Which wasn't to say she wouldn't give it a damn good try!

She gave an uninterested shrug. 'When I went to school the other children quickly latched onto the fact that my initial was J. followed by Nixon, and when you say the two of them together…' She trailed off pointedly, giving him a sideways glance. 'You aren't coming home with me, you know.'

Of course he knew. After the last two months of sending letters to her father, just in the hopes of being able to meet him and discuss the movie rights to his book, of the use of a PO box for that correspondence, of the author never agreeing to so much as meeting with his own publisher, it would be expecting too much now for his daughter to just take Nik home with her and introduce the two men.

'You mentioned earlier that your father isn't well…?' he said instead.

She stiffened, all expression suddenly erased from her face. 'I mentioned it, yes,' she acknowledged guardedly.

'Nothing life-threatening, I hope?' Nik persisted.

'It depends on what you call life-threatening,' she returned evasively, a frown now marring her creamy brow.

He shrugged, having an idea that in the case of Jackson I. Nixon the writing and subsequent success of *No Ordinary Boy* didn't fit in too well with his other literary achievements. Nik didn't happen to agree with him, and neither did the millions of other people who had bought and enjoyed the book, but that was just his opinion…

His mouth twisted wryly. 'It usually means resulting in premature death.'

'Mr Prince—okay, Nik,' Jinx conceded impatiently as he scowled his displeasure at the formality. 'Just stay away from my father, okay?' Her expression was fierce with emotion now.

'But I only want—'

'I know what you want, Nik!' Her eyes flashed deeply purple in the illumination of the street lamp, her tiny hands clenched into fists at her sides. 'You want to make a film of *No Ordinary Boy*. In the hopes, no doubt, of adding yet another Oscar to the five you already have in your trophy cabinet!'

God, this woman was beautiful when roused, whether to anger or passion. And at this moment Nik knew exactly which one he wanted it to be!

'Perhaps I should feel flattered that you know I have five Oscars—'

'And perhaps you shouldn't!'

'Another Oscar would be nice,' he conceded huskily. 'But at this moment I'm damned if I wouldn't settle for a night in bed with you!'

Colour flared suddenly in the paleness of her cheeks, her lips full and inviting, her breasts moving with the same rapidity of her breathing.

'I wasn't aware that was an option,' she retorted, the nerve pulsing in her raised jaw giving lie to that challenge.

Because Nik was experienced enough to know that, no matter how she might try to deny it—and she was denying it!—Jinx was as physically aware of him as he was of her.

'Not as an instead of, no,' he admitted gruffly, moving closer to her, not quite touching, but nevertheless feeling the heat given off from her body. He reached up to touch the pouting softness of her mouth, feeling the quiver his caress invoked. 'You want me too, Jinx,' he said with certainty.

Her eyes were so dark now they appeared black, her mouth trembling moistly, a becoming flush to her cheeks, the hardened nubs at the tips of the gentle sweep of her breasts visible beneath the thin material of her dress. And Nik was sure, if he could have touched the very centre of her desire, that she would be moist there too, as ready for him as he was for her.

And they hadn't so much as kissed each other yet!

But that was easily rectified, Nik decided, no longer able to resist the urge to take her into his arms, to mould her body fiercely against his, to let her feel the surge of his desire against her warm thighs, before he bent his head and his mouth took hers—and his previously well-constructed world fell apart!

Drowning.

It was like drowning.

Every other woman he had ever known was instantly consigned to a black void and could never be recalled. Only Jinx existed, only the touch, the warmth, the smell, the taste of her.

This woman, this tiny, stubborn, five-foot delicacy of a woman, was taking possession of him, body and soul…!

CHAPTER THREE

WHAT was she doing?

Whatever it was, Jinx knew she couldn't stop it. Not yet. Oh, please, not yet!

Nik was kissing her as if he wanted to make her a part of him, to devour her, to take her completely inside him. Or for him to be completely inside her. His thighs were moving restlessly against hers, rubbing, tormenting, frustrating, until Jinx wanted nothing more than to throw off all their clothes and be taken by him right now, the two of them lost in the heat of the sexual arousal that drew them nearer and nearer to a climax that was completely beyond their control.

'Let's go to a hotel!' Nik managed to take his lips from hers long enough to groan achingly, long hands framing her face as he looked down at her with glittering silver eyes. 'I don't know what you're doing to me, Jinx Nixon, but if I don't make love to you soon then I'm going to self-combust!'

She knew it, could feel the force of his need. A need she easily matched.

'Feel it, Jinx.' Nik's thighs moved erotically against her, hard, pulsing with desire.

A desire that made her own thighs moist, burning, aching, throbbing with a need that she knew would explode if Nik's flesh should so much as touch hers.

But she couldn't just book into a hotel with a man—*especially* not this man! And while her body might think

40

that it recognized and knew his, she knew she had every reason to distrust him. More reasons than he realized.

'No!' Nik protested as he seemed to feel her moving emotionally away from him, his arms tightening about her as he tried to hold onto the moment. 'Jinx, I know you want me too!' he groaned.

Oh, yes, she wanted him. But she would never give in to that want—she had too much to lose if she ever did.

She straightened determinedly away from him. 'And do you always get what you want, Nik?' She sighed.

'Almost always,' he confirmed, his arms falling back to his sides.

'Then a little self-denial could be good for you.'

'It isn't self-denial, it's Jinx-denial,' he corrected huskily. 'And men have been known to go insane trying to draw back from the brink you just took me to!' His eyes glittered with the intensity of his feelings.

'Women too, or so I'm told,' she came back dryly, some of her own normal reserve returning now that she was no longer held in his arms. Although the desire he had aroused hadn't abated in the slightest...

'Then why—'

'Because it would be a mistake!' she cried frustratedly. 'Can't you understand?' she continued as he looked at her blankly. 'You are positively the last man on earth I ever want to become involved with!'

He became very still, his expression guarded now, a shutter coming down over grey eyes, his mouth a grim line. 'Because I want to make a movie of *No Ordinary Boy*?'

'Because you want to film *No Ordinary Boy*,' she agreed flatly.

'Damn it, woman—'

'Nik, swearing at me isn't going to help this situation one little bit—'

'Maybe not,' he admitted grimly. 'But it makes me feel a hell of a lot better!'

She gave him a bleak smile. 'I'm sure it does,' she conceded. 'But it isn't going to change a thing. Because I'm not stupid enough to go to a hotel or anywhere else with you. Neither do I have any intention of taking you home with me—'

'You really are the most stubborn—'

'And if you attempt to follow me home,' Jinx continued as if he hadn't spoken, 'then I shall contact the police and have you arrested for stalking me.'

'Wouldn't that rather null and void this phobia you have about your father's privacy?' he mocked. 'I'm quite well known, Jinx; there is no way having me arrested wouldn't appear in some tabloid newspaper or other.'

Nik Prince's much-photographed face and highly recognizable profile were aspects of this situation that she was well aware of. They were yet more reasons she intended avoiding him at all costs.

'That's your problem, not mine,' she dismissed with much more confidence than she actually felt. 'My priority is to keep any publicity from even touching my father. It's the reason a pseudonym was used, for heaven's sake!' Her eyes flashed warningly.

Nik's frown deepened. 'What exactly is wrong with your father?'

Jinx turned away. 'Just stay away from us, Nik.'

'And if I can't do that?' he challenged.

She shrugged. 'Watch this space.'

'Damn it, he wrote the book; surely it must have occurred to him, to both of you, that it might be a bestseller—'

'Of course it didn't occur to us!' Jinx protested heatedly, the colour back in her cheeks now. 'Writing a book is a very personal thing.' She shook her head. 'Who could possibly have imagined that *No Ordinary Boy* would be as popular as it was?'

'As it still is.'

'Yes,' she conceded quietly.

'Aren't you being just a little selfish, Jinx?' he pursued relentlessly. 'You've made your own feelings about my filming *No Ordinary Boy* more than clear, but until I've actually spoken to him I have no way of knowing that's your father's opinion too...'

Jinx looked up at him, tears glittering in her deep blue eyes.

'Why don't you just leave us alone?' she choked.

'Because I can't do that.'

One of the tears spilled over onto her cheek and she immediately brushed it away. 'How I wish none of this had ever happened!'

'Oh, come on, Jinx,' he scorned. 'All that money your father is earning has to have its advantages for you too. That dress you're wearing, the diamond earrings—'

'That's enough!' she exclaimed.

'Quite enough,' he agreed.

'I bought these things myself,' she told him angrily. 'With my own money. Earned by my own endeavours.'

'If you say so.'

'I do,' she snapped.

'Fine,' he replied.

Jinx looked up at him searchingly, knowing by the determined glitter in his eyes that he wasn't the sort of man to back off just because she asked him to. Considering the lengths she knew he must have gone to in order to meet her this evening, she shouldn't be surprised by that.

And she wasn't. Surprise certainly wasn't her primary emotion.

'If I so much as *think* you're following me home I *will* contact the police, Nik,' she declared.

He gave an inclination of his head. 'I know that.'

'And?'

'And I'll find some other way,' he answered unhesitantly.

Looking at him, she could see that he would, as he had arranged their meeting this evening, by fair means or foul.

'I have to go,' she told him coldly.

He shrugged. 'Your prerogative.'

She suddenly realized from the harshness of his expression, that whatever had happened between them a few minutes ago was definitely over now as far as he was concerned.

Which was what she had wanted. Wasn't it…?

Of course it was. Any relationship with Nik Prince was dangerous. To her own peace of mind, as well as her father's.

She nodded abruptly before turning and walking away, knowing from the way she felt no tingling of awareness down her spine that Nik wasn't watching her this time. And why should he? He had failed in his objective, which meant she was of no further use to him.

What would Nik say, Jinx wondered, if he were to ever learn the truth?

He was less than proud of himself, Nik acknowledged uncomfortably as he sat across the dinner table from Jane Morrow, the pretty blonde thirtyish-year-old making no effort to hide the attraction she felt towards him, touching him constantly as they talked.

The last six days of searching for Jinx's home address had proved even more frustrating than the previous two months.

There were several J. Nixons listed in the London telephone books, none of them the right ones. Jackson Nixon's previous publishers—of those serious historical tomes—had informed him that Professor Nixon had recently moved and hadn't yet supplied them with his new address. Although, they had also added firmly, they wouldn't have been able to reveal that information even if they did have it!

Nik hadn't been any more successful when he'd decided to turn his attention to investigating Jinx instead of her father.

Cambridge University had been of no use at all in supplying him with an address for Dr Juliet Nixon, claiming they weren't at liberty to give out that information, although they had offered to forward any letter he cared to send to Dr Nixon at the university. Very helpful!

A visit to Jinx's friend Susan Fellows two days after her party, on the pretext that he had lost a cufflink on Saturday evening, had proved totally unfruitful, both with regard to the non-existent cufflink and in garnering any information on Jinx. Apart from confirming that, yes, the Nixons had moved in the last year—with no address forthcoming, naturally!—and that Jinx's father had been ill for some time, the beautiful blonde hadn't wanted to discuss her friend at all.

None of Stazy's friends seemed to know Jinx personally, let alone where she lived. Which had brought Nik full circle and left his only possible source of information to be Jane Morrow at Stephens Publishing…

But, strangely enough, even though he had felt no qualms about calculatingly charming this woman a month ago, he now felt distaste at the possibility of taking it any further. As Jane seemed to want him to do. Oh, Jane was attractive enough, but his reason for asking her out again was certainly less than honourable.

Honourable…

Now there was a word to be reckoned with, Nik acknowledged self-derisively. Was he an honourable man? He had always thought so. But his behaviour these last few weeks concerning meeting Jackson Nixon was certainly questionable. In fact, since meeting Jinx, it seemed to have become something of an obsession with him.

As had Jinx!

In fact, Nik had found himself thinking altogether too much about Jinx Nixon the last six days, about the way she had felt in his arms that night, and not enough about her father, and the movie he wanted to make of the man's book.

'—had some really good news today.' His attention returned to Jane Morrow as she spoke excitedly, her almost boyish slenderness due to the nervous energy that marked all of her quick movements.

'Tell me about it,' he invited.

'J. I. Watson sent in his second manuscript this morning!' Jane told him, her face flushed with the triumph of being able to tell him that. 'James has it, so I haven't had the chance to read all of it yet, but the little I have tells me it's going to be another runaway success. Which doesn't always happen with second books, you know…'

'Is it another *No Ordinary Boy* book?' he asked.

'Oh, yes,' Jane confirmed. 'Of course, it won't have that title, but it has all the same characters, and…'

She continued to talk, but Nik had faded her out after

her initial announcement that they had received the second J. I. Watson 'Boy' manuscript.

Was Jinx aware that her father had written a second book? From her vehemence on Saturday evening concerning the commercial success of the first one, he would have thought she would rather her father never put fictional pen to paper again. Or fingers to keyboard, depending on which method Jackson Nixon preferred to use in order to write his books, Nik allowed ruefully.

But this second manuscript made it even more urgent that he meet the other man; the publication of the second book, coinciding with the possible release of the movie of the first book, would be tremendous publicity for all concerned.

If only he could get past Jinx and talk to her father!

'I suppose he's requested the same conditions as before?' he quizzed Jane lightly, knowing she had been as puzzled by the author's behaviour as James Stephens was.

In fact, Nik having learnt that the J in the author's name stood for Jackson, the I for Ivor meant that he probably now knew more about the author than the publishers did!

Jane made a face. 'No publicity? No interviews? No book signings?' She nodded. 'Pretty much. Except there was rather an interesting footnote this time…' She broke off teasingly as she gave him a pointed look.

Nik moved uncomfortably under that predatory gaze. 'Yes…?'

'Well, it's strange, really,' Jane confided huskily, once again touching his hand. 'You're actually mentioned by name too this time.'

He stiffened warily. 'I am?'

'"Absolutely no further correspondence from Nik

Prince to be forwarded on'' was how I believe it was worded.' She gave him an assessing look. 'I think you must have really upset him with all your approaches regarding making the film.'

No, he hadn't upset Jackson Nixon—how could he have done when it was virtually impossible to meet the man? The person who was so annoyed with him was his daughter, Jinx. And Nik wasn't altogether sure that it was a totally impersonal annoyance, either.

There was no getting away from the fact that the two of them had had an explosive response to each other on Saturday evening. In fact, in any other circumstances, Nik was sure his pursuit of Jinx Nixon would have culminated in the most passionate affair he had ever been involved in. Something he was sure Jinx had been only too aware of, too.

Jackson Nixon's adamant refusal now to have any further contact with Nik, he was sure, had been instigated by his daughter's reluctance to have any further contact with him!

Making Nik all the more determined that he wouldn't back off, either from Jackson Nixon or his beautiful daughter. The sooner he got Jinx into his bed, the easier this might all be resolved! In fact, just the thought of that slenderly curvaceous body curled nakedly in his arms was enough to arouse him.

Which accounted for the reason, he told himself, that he felt so reluctant to accept Jane Morrow's invitation to join her for coffee when he took her back to her apartment later that evening. 'Coffee' in this case, he knew, was really Jane's way of inviting him into her bed—something, for all her touching and innuendos, he had so far managed to avoid. And intended continuing to do so!

Because at the moment all of his desire was centred on a tiny, rebellious redhead with violet-blue eyes...

He gave a regretful shake of his head. 'Perhaps another time; I have a really early appointment in the morning that I need to be fully awake and alert for,' he invented to nullify any insult Jane might feel at his refusal.

Jane moved closer towards him, her hand resting lightly on his chest as she looked up at him, her tongue moving suggestively across her lips. 'I'll make sure to set my alarm,' she persisted.

'I really can't, Jane.' He smiled to take the edge off his rejection.

'Why not?' She frowned her disappointment, her smile fading. 'Or is it that I've served my purpose now that I've told you as much about J. I. Watson as I know?' she guessed astutely, eyes starting to glitter with anger.

She was too close to the truth for Nik's comfort, he acknowledged self-disgustedly. He also didn't like that slightly possessive edge he detected in her tone; a couple of dinners together certainly did not give her that right. 'I truly am sorry—'

'Not as sorry as I am.' Her voice was sharp with fury.

Nik didn't like her tone at all now, finding it slightly threatening. It only confirmed his decision that to have pursued any further sort of relationship with this woman would have been a mistake.

However, he also knew that his own reluctance wasn't entirely due to any noble sentiment on his part—it had more to do with the haunting memory of a pair of violet-blue eyes, poutingly kissable lips, and a slenderly seductive body.

Although Jane Morrow was already angry enough at his reluctance to share her bed, without knowing that he was actually attracted to the daughter of J. I. Watson!

'Hell hath no fury'…and all that, Nik thought with an inner wince.

Jane's pretty face was no longer pretty at all. 'I should have known that Nik Prince wouldn't really be interested in me, but rather in what I might be able to tell him about the elusive J. I. Watson!' She gave a disgusted shake of her head, agitatedly searching through her evening bag for her apartment key now. 'Well, if it's any consolation,' she bit out, having found the key at last and unlocked the door, 'I have a feeling the reason J. I. Watson shuns the limelight may be because he has—slightly feminine tendencies, shall we be kind and say?'

Nik, having been about to apologize yet again, became suddenly still instead, his eyes narrowing. 'What makes you say that?'

She shrugged too-narrow shoulders as she paused in the open doorway. 'Either that or someone else writes his letters for him; the last two we've received definitely had a female perfume about them.'

Jinx's perfume…?

That elusive, but at the same time heady perfume of Lily of the Valley that he had commented on on Saturday and that Jinx had so summarily dismissed?

'Did you recognize—'

'No, I didn't!' Jane turned to glare at him indignantly, her face twisted in anger now. 'You really are all that they accuse you of in the press, aren't you?' she accused scornfully.

Arrogant. Hard. Cold. Calculating. Single-minded. Brilliant. Gifted. He really had lost track of the names the press had bestowed on him over the years, rarely read anything they wrote about him nowadays, although he did know that the latter two comments were usually the exception to the rule. Most reporters preferred to dwell on his cold arrogance or the latest woman in his life rather than the skill that had earned him those five Oscars Jinx had referred to so scathingly on Saturday evening.

Jinx, again…

He really was becoming obsessed, wasn't he? Although, what Jane said about the perfume on those last two letters was interesting. More than interesting, in fact. Perhaps, as he was reported to have been ill for some time now, Jackson Nixon had had more than a little help from his daughter in the writing of *No Ordinary Boy*? Perhaps—

Nik froze as another—totally amazing!—alternative suddenly occurred to him.

No—it couldn't be!

They couldn't all have been so wrong.

Could they…?

CHAPTER FOUR

'JULIET INDIA NIXON.'

The name, softly but firmly spoken by Nik Prince as he sat opposite Jinx in the lounge of this large, impersonal London hotel, hung in the air between them like a dark, threatening cloud.

Or maybe that was only the way it seemed to her, Jinx allowed heavily; after all, Nik had absolutely no reason to feel in the least threatened by this meeting. In fact, the opposite, she would have thought.

As evidenced by his air of satisfaction as he leant further over the coffee-table that divided them, that silver gaze easily holding hers as he murmured, 'That is you, isn't it, Jinx?'

She forced herself to turn calmly away from those all-seeing eyes, not in the least surprised to see the woman sitting alone two tables down in this hotel lounge staring avidly at Nik Prince; he was the sort of man who attracted female attention wherever he went! Not that Nik seemed at all aware of that interested female gaze—no, all of his attention was firmly fixed on her.

Jinx gave the other woman a sympathetic smile before turning away, deliberately adding sugar to one of the two cappuccinos they had ordered, to give herself a little time before answering Nik.

Not that she thought for a moment that time was going to be of any help to her whatsoever; it had already been two days—two excruciatingly tense days!—since the letter had arrived in the post office box from Nik Prince with, 'Juliet India Nixon or just J. I. Watson? I think we need to talk, don't you? Reception, The Waldorf, Wednesday at 10.30 a.m.' written on it. And Jinx was no further now towards knowing how to deal with this forcefully determined man than she had been then!

She could try continuing to bluff her way out of it, of course, although she didn't hold out much hope of this astutely intelligent man putting up with that for too long. She could try telling him the truth and appealing to his better nature—but did he have a 'better nature'? The press seemed to think not—and, judging by his tenacity in tracking her down this last week, Jinx was inclined to agree with them.

Her chin rose slightly. 'What do you want from me?'

Silver eyes gleamed. 'The truth, of course.'

Her mouth twisted contemptuously. 'Would you know that if it were to jump up and bite you on the nose?'

That silver gleam became slightly opaque now as his gaze narrowed. 'Tell me, is this dislike personal, or just a general one towards movie directors?'

A week ago she would have said the latter, but Nik's behaviour over the last week and a half hadn't endeared him to her in the slightest. 'Tell me, Mr Prince, exactly how did you come to the conclusion that I am J. I. Watson, rather than your initial assumption that it was my father?' She made no effort to keep the derision from her voice.

He looked so much in control sitting across from her, so sure of himself, so—so damned arrogant. Because he was arrogant. And ruthless. A man who didn't care about the how or why, as long as he got what he wanted. And this week he wanted to meet J. I. Watson. In fact, he believed that was exactly what he was doing.

She had no intention of telling him how wrong he was…

But even now, disliking him as much as she did, it was impossible to deny that just looking at him, so self-assured in casual trousers and a cream silk shirt, made her pulse race, sent a shiver of awareness down the length of her spine.

It had been this way since she'd first looked at him at Susan and Leo's party. This complete awareness, just his gaze resting on her mouth—as it was now!—making her feel as if he had actually touched her there, caressed her.

'Does it matter how I found out?' He shrugged those powerful shoulders dismissively. 'It is you, isn't it?' It was a statement rather than a question.

How to answer that?

She had never expected to have to answer questions like this. Because she had never thought the book would become such a runaway bestseller, with cries from all directions for the appearance of the author. And an offer to buy the film rights from such a prestigious director as Nik Prince…

He was still and silent as he waited for her to answer him, like a stalking tiger with his prey, that silver gaze almost hypnotic.

Jinx gave a deliberate smile, if only to show him that she wasn't in the least mesmerised. Or in the least daunted by the fact that he believed he had discovered her real identity. 'And what if it is?' she evaded. 'Surely I've made it more than obvious that I'm even less interested in your offer for the film rights than my father would have been?'

He arched one dark brow. 'You haven't heard my offer yet.'

'Because I don't need to.' She gave a shake of her

head, red hair silkily vibrant. 'I've said no. Several times. As James Stephens has obviously informed you.'

Nik Prince once again sat forward in his chair, seeming to fill the whole of Jinx's vision now. 'What are you so afraid of, Jinx? Maybe if you tell me that—'

'You'll give up on the idea for the film and just go away?' she scorned.

'Well, no…I couldn't exactly say that,' he conceded wryly.

'I thought not,' she rasped.

'But I might be able to understand your stubborn refusal a little more,' he continued.

'Really?' Jinx gave a disbelieving snort. 'And why do you imagine that I need your understanding?'

He drew in a harsh breath, his expression grim now, eyes narrowed, lips thinned. 'Right now, taking your paranoia into account, what you need is my silence, young lady,' he rapped. 'Let's go from there, shall we?'

'Are you threatening me, Mr Prince?' she said slowly, replacing her cup and saucer back on the table.

'No, I'm—' He gave an exasperated sigh. 'No, Jinx, I'm not threatening you—'

'It certainly sounded as if you were.' She met his gaze unflinchingly.

Nik gave a sigh of obvious frustration. 'I didn't ask for this meeting with you today in order to argue with you—'

'You didn't ask for this meeting at all, Mr Prince— you demanded it,' she reminded him forcefully. 'And you did it with the belief that you had the leverage to talk me into allowing you to purchase the film rights of *No Ordinary Boy*. So how do you think you're doing so far?'

'Badly,' he conceded heavily.

'Very badly,' she confirmed.

'That's because you—' He broke off, staring at her impatiently. 'Jinx, what do you have against the movie being made?'

'By you?' she delayed.

'By anyone.'

How astute of him to realize that her stubbornness really wasn't personal, that she would have been just as adamant in her refusal concerning the approach of any film company.

Although she had to say, since meeting Nik Prince, her determination had grown where he was concerned.

Because she recognized his powerful force? Because she knew he wasn't a man who took no for an answer? Or was it simply that the fierce attraction she felt towards him, from that first moment of meeting him at Susan and Leo's, made her doubly wary?

She couldn't remember the last time she had felt attracted to any man, let alone one as forcefully compelling as Nik Prince. She had a good idea where such an attraction could lead if she allowed it to. Which was why she was determined to hold this man, in particular, completely at arm's length.

'Jinx?'

She looked across at him, frowning as she tried to remember what his last question had been. 'Have you read *No Ordinary Boy*?'

His expression darkened. 'Well, of course I've read it! The whole damn world has read it—'

'I think that's somewhat of an exaggeration,' she scoffed.

'It's been published in over ninety countries, in twenty-five languages—'

'Having received one set of royalties already, I do have all that information,' she cut in.

'Then you must also realize that the majority of the people who have read the book believe that J. I. Watson is a man—'

'As you did,' she pointed out.

'As I did,' he agreed. 'The book is about a twelve-year-old boy confined to a wheelchair who suddenly discovers he has super mental abilities—'

'I know what the book's about, thank you! But you think me incapable of imagining being a twelve-year-old boy?' she challenged, her unease increasing if that should prove to be the case.

That silver gaze swept over her with slow deliberation, lingering on the curve of her breasts in the cream silk blouse, before moving down the slender length of her legs in fitted black trousers.

Again, it was almost as if he touched her, as if those big, capable hands had actually caressed her, leaving heat wherever they touched.

'I think,' he finally said huskily, 'that you might have trouble imagining being a boy of any age!'

Her heart gave a leap at the warmth she could see in his eyes, the complete awareness of her treacherous body making her answer him sharply. 'How typically sexist of you, Mr Prince!'

He shrugged broad shoulders. 'Not at all, Jinx.' It seemed he deliberately used her nickname, the name only close friends used. 'Merely stating it as I see it.'

'Well, it would appear that you see it wrong, wouldn't it?' she taunted.

He looked at her with narrowed eyes now. 'It would appear so...' he slowly echoed her words.

Too much, Jinx, she reprimanded herself, she had said far too much; she wanted this man completely out of her

life and that of *No Ordinary Boy*, not to make him all
the more curious about its author!

She shook her head. 'I simply don't believe that the
book would transfer to the big screen.'

He looked derisive now. 'You don't?'

Her cheeks flushed angrily at what she sensed was his
amusement at her lack of faith in his ability as a film
director. Oh, she knew all about this man's successes, the
awards, the Oscars—just as she knew that *No Ordinary
Boy* was so personal to her that she couldn't allow a third
party to rip it apart in order to make a 'marketable' film.

'No, I don't,' she snapped.

'Why don't you let me be the judge of what does and
doesn't transfer to the big screen?'

He was laughing at her, damn him. When she found
little or nothing about this situation in the least amusing.
'My answer is no, Mr Prince,' she told him with finality,
bending to pick up her bag from the carpeted floor. 'It
will remain no.'

She was leaving!

This tiny slip of a woman, with ice in her eyes and
fire in her hair, was walking out on him!

That definitely had to be a first...

He had thought at the weekend, once he had estab-
lished that Juliet India Nixon was more probably the author of *No Ordinary Boy* than her father, that he finally
had her at a disadvantage, that it would simply be a case
of meeting with her today to tie up the loose ends regarding the movie rights. But Jinx Nixon was anything
but amenable, was just as determined as she ever had
been to thwart him.

'Just what is it with you, Jinx?' he challenged as she
stood up. 'Could it be that it's beneath the highbrow Dr

Juliet Nixon to be associated with a work of fiction like *No Ordinary Boy*?'

If he had thought her eyes cold before, they now turned to fire, her beautiful face flushed with the same anger as she flicked that blazing red hair back over one slender shoulder to glare down at him.

Nik had hoped to evoke some sort of response by his challenge—he just hadn't been quite prepared for the one he got.

This woman was so beautiful when roused, so vibrantly alive, that he immediately saw her aroused in a completely different way, the image of her lying naked and wanton in his arms causing him to shift uncomfortably as his body responded to that image.

It was totally amazing; he hadn't physically responded like this just at the thought of a woman in his bed since his college days, but ten minutes in Jinx Nixon's company and he was doing exactly that.

Something, given the circumstances, he stood about as much chance of achieving where Jinx was concerned as flying to the moon!

He grimaced. 'I apologize for that remark.' He sighed, shaking his head. 'I just don't understand you.' Something else that hadn't happened in a long time.

Perhaps he had become jaded over the years, too accustomed to women wanting something from him, from the power he wielded as head of PrinceMovies, but nothing he said or did seemed to make any difference whatsoever to Jinx's resolve not to have anything to do with him or his movie company. By itself that was enough to frustrate the hell out of him, but taking his personal—physical!—response to this woman into account, it only made the situation more explosive.

Jinx seemed to be confused herself now, as if she wasn't quite sure what to do next, either.

Nik knew exactly what she wanted to do—tell him goodbye and walk out of here!—but he could also see by the perplexed frown of indecision on her creamy brow that something was holding her back from doing that.

What could it be?

What was this woman still hiding from him?

God, he was arrogant, wasn't he? Nik recognized with self-disgust. There must be any number of things this woman wasn't telling him. Probably not just him either; Jinx Nixon came over as a very private person, indeed. In fact, he had a feeling Jinx was the sort of woman it could take a lifetime to get to know.

Hell! It was dangerous to even think about the words 'Jinx' and 'lifetime' in the same sentence. It wasn't that he was particularly anti-commitment; after all, his parents had been happily married right up until the day his father had died, and his sister Stazy was certainly happy in her marriage; it just wasn't an option Nik had ever considered for himself.

So why was he considering it now?

He wasn't, came the blunt answer. Not seriously. Damn it, he barely knew Jinx Nixon, and the little he did know, that she was stubborn, sassy and highly intellectual, totally nullified the fact that she was so incredibly beautiful.

Nevertheless, Nik still had a feeling, for his own self-preservation, that the idea of seduction was no longer an option where this woman was concerned.

'Please sit down again, Jinx,' he persuaded, still sensing her indecision.

She sat, looking down at her hands now, the fiery curtain of her hair falling forward to caress the paleness of her cheeks as those hands clenched tightly together.

What was it? What had he missed? Because Nik was more convinced than ever that he was missing something, that he just had to find the right button to press and Jinx Nixon would be like putty in his hands. He just had no idea what that button was!

'Jinx, will you have dinner with me this evening?'

Now where the hell had that come from? Nik wondered dazedly. The idea hadn't even formed in his mind, let alone been processed for viability—if it had he would have told himself what a bad idea it was for him to spend any more time alone with Jinx, that he just wanted her signature on a contract and then he would be on his way.

She was looking at him now, her head tilted thoughtfully to one side, a slight smile curving that deeply kissable mouth. 'You didn't mean to say that...'

'No,' he admitted with a wry smile. 'But having said it...?'

She laughed softly, a huskily evocative sound. 'I don't think that's a good idea, Nik.'

Neither did he—just the sound of his name on her lips was enough to send a sliver of awareness down the length of his spine. 'Perhaps not,' he conceded. 'But I'm asking, anyway.'

How his two brothers would laugh if they could see him now—the arrogantly self-contained Nik willing this tiny woman to have dinner with him tonight. Zak and Rik would find it highly amusing that he had to ask twice at all, let alone exert all of his pressure of will in order to get the positive answer he wanted.

And he did want it. That cautious self-preservation told him to stay as far away from this woman as it was possible for him to be, but all of his natural instincts told him he wanted to be with her again. That he wanted so much more than that.

And he wasn't averse to using every means at his disposal to achieve his objective!

'Surely your father won't mind your going out and leaving him for one evening?' he prompted softly, closely watching her response to this mention of her father, knowing by the way her expression suddenly became blankly unreadable that he had touched a raw nerve. 'Just how ill is your father, Jinx?' he pressed at her continuing silence.

She seemed to flinch at his persistence, her smile having faded long ago, once again withdrawing behind that coolly dismissive mask. 'I have no intention of discussing my father with you, Nik,' she snapped. 'Either now or at any other time,' she added firmly.

In other words, she wasn't going to have dinner with him this evening. Damn. Good move, Nik! He cursed his own stupidity in having moved too far, too fast. So much for his finding the right buttons to press...

'I heard that he had some sort of nervous breakdown a year or so ago?' he murmured, still sure that Jackson Nixon was the key to this woman's acquiescence.

Then why did he feel such a heel as her face paled even more, her eyes huge blue pools of pain and confusion as she looked at him incredulously?

'And where, exactly, did you *hear* that?' she demanded, her whole body defensively taut as she sat up straighter in the chair, those tiny breasts unknowingly thrust provocatively forward.

A fact that Nik tried his best to ignore—and failed miserably, able to see the outline of her nipples against the silky fabric of her blouse; indeed, almost able to discern their rosy hue. 'One of his colleagues at the university mentioned—'

'You had *no* right to go anywhere near my father's colleagues!' She gasped. 'This is *exactly* what I didn't want! *Exactly* what I knew would happen once people started snooping about in an effort to meet the author of *No Ordinary Boy*!' Two bright spots of colour had appeared in the paleness of her cheeks as she breathed deeply in her agitation. 'Stay away from my father, Nik! Stay away from anyone who knows him! Most of all—' she stood up again forcefully '—stay away from me!'

He couldn't do that. Didn't want to do that. More than ever he wanted this woman to have dinner with him this evening. Forget dinner—he just wanted her with him this evening.

'Jinx, please sit down—'

'No way,' she told him angrily, once again flicking back the fiery length of her hair. 'I can't believe you did such a thing! Can't believe anyone could sink so low as to—'

'You weren't exactly cooperating,' Nik pointed out as he stood up to face her.

Jinx looked at him incredulously. 'And that was enough for you to pry into my private life, my father's private life, like some cheap—'

'Excuse me, Mr Prince—it is Nik Prince, isn't it?'

Nik had turned sharply at the first sound of the female voice, his angry gaze narrowing warily as he took in the woman's appearance—short dark hair, deep brown eyes, a pleasantly smiling mouth—as she looked at him enquiringly.

'The film director?' the woman pressed brightly.

Nik felt the faint stirrings of unease; in his experience there was only one profession he knew of who pushed their way into other people's lives in this intrusive way. And as he saw the woman nod to a man who had just entered the lounge, the familiar camera slung about his neck, Nik knew that his guess had been the correct one.

Hell, Jinx was skittish enough already, without finding herself face to face with a reporter and her photographer!

CHAPTER FIVE

'WHAT do you think you're doing?' Jinx squeaked indignantly as she suddenly found her arm grasped in Nik Prince's vice-like fingers as he began marching her across the room. 'Nik—'

'Move!' he instructed harshly as she attempted to push his hand away from her arm.

'But I don't—' Jinx broke off in alarm as a light was suddenly flashed in her face, momentarily blinding her.

Nik just kept on walking, pulling the semi-blinded Jinx along with him.

What on earth was going on? she wondered dazedly. Who was that woman? The same woman who had been staring at Nik so avidly across the lounge earlier…! Why had Nik wanted to get away from her so quickly? Most puzzling of all, what had been the source of that light that had blinded her?

'She was a reporter, Jinx,' Nik told her as he pulled her into the lift and pressed the button to ascend.

But not before another light had flashed brightly, almost in their faces this time, Jinx able to see clearly that the flash had come from a camera being thrust between the rapidly closing lift doors.

'And he—' Nik reached out to grab the camera just as the doors closed, the other man's cry of protest instantly cut off mid-flow '—is her associate!' He released Jinx to open the back of the camera and take out the film and thrust it into his trouser pocket. 'Damn, damn, damn!' he muttered grimly as he closed the camera.

A reporter…

Not just a reporter. Paparazzi!

The scourge of the true reporter, whose aim was to report the real news, these other, less professional members of the press weren't really looking for truth, but went in search of sensationalism.

Jinx felt slightly sick at the realization that she had been in the presence of just such a reporter the last half an hour or so, that she had been completely wrong in her assumption earlier that the other woman had been looking at Nik because she'd recognized him and found him attractive; this woman was out for a story, and didn't particularly care how she got it.

Her teeth began to chatter uncontrollably in reaction to what had just happened.

If Nik hadn't realized— If he hadn't spotted the photographer— If he hadn't grabbed the camera in that way—!

'It's okay, Jinx.' Nik spoke soothingly as he moved to stand in front of her, touching her gently as he moved the fringe of hair back from over her horrified eyes. 'It's okay,' he repeated encouragingly.

Of course it wasn't okay. Nik was a personality, a highly photographic one, and if he hadn't retrieved that film then Jinx knew she would have appeared beside him in a photograph in one of tomorrow's newspapers—probably with a speculative comment about who this latest mystery woman was in his life. After that, it would only be a matter of time…!

'Come on,' he urged as the lift doors opened.

Jinx followed him out of the lift, only to come to an abrupt halt as she saw they were on one of the upper floors. A floor containing bedrooms, she realized as a maid came out from cleaning one of them.

'Could you see that this is taken down to Reception and returned to its owner?' Nik handed the camera over to the rather surprised maid. 'You can't miss him—he's the one who looks as if he just found a cent but lost a dollar,' he added with grim satisfaction before turning back to Jinx.

A Jinx who stared back at him accusingly. This was all his fault—

'This isn't my fault, Jinx.' His words harshly echoed what she was thinking.

Her eyes widened. 'Then whose fault is it? Mine?' she asked scornfully. 'Reporters and their photographers don't usually follow me around, I can assure you—'

'They would if they knew you were J. I. Watson!' he assured her scathingly before turning to open the door across the corridor, standing back to allow her to enter first.

Jinx hung back reluctantly. Did she really want to compound this situation by going into a hotel bedroom with Nik Prince—?

'Jinx, it's my guess it isn't going to be safe for you to leave here for some time yet,' Nik informed her dryly as he saw her obvious reluctance. 'In fact, I may have to have some help in creating a diversion.'

'I beg your pardon?' Jinx queried as she marched past him.

Into what turned out not to be the bedroom she had been expecting, but a sitting-room obviously attached to a bedroom. Of course; she should have known that a man like Nik Prince would have a suite, not just a bedroom!

'Don't worry about it, Jinx,' Nik reassured her as he strode across the room to pick up the telephone receiver. 'I'll sort this out in just—'

'Don't *worry* about it?' she repeated with suppressed

violence as she threw her shoulder bag down onto one of the sofas. '*You'll* sort it out? It's because of you that I'm in this mess in the first place!' She glared across the room at him, eyes gleaming deeply blue, her cheeks flushed. 'Did you organize for that reporter to be there? Is this some trick to force me into giving you the film rights to *No Ordinary Boy*?'

'Of course not,' Nik rasped.

'I don't believe you!' Jinx dissolved into floods of tears, her face buried in her hands.

As if by doing so she could shut out Nik Prince altogether, could fool herself into believing none of this were really happening!

'Jinx, it was me the reporter spoke to, not you,' he reminded her. 'It was me she was after, not you.'

'Are you sure?' She so much needed to believe him!

His expression softened, and he murmured her name as he took her into his arms. Arms that felt strong and protective as they completely enveloped her, and Jinx reacted instinctively as she clung to him like a rock in a storm. A storm that seemed to be gaining momentum and force with each passing second.

'Jinx…!' This time her name was a husky groan, one of Nik's arms tightening about the slenderness of her waist, the other hand moving to cup her chin as he raised her face to his, his eyes looking deeply into hers as he slowly lowered his head.

There was only time for the briefest moment of doubt, before she gave herself up to the seductive claim of his mouth on hers.

Emotions swirled and grew as she kissed him back with all the pent-up feelings inside her, her lips parting beneath the pressure of his, senses leaping as he began a slow exploration with the tip of his tongue, first along the edge of her bottom lip, then the moist softness within.

His arms tightened as Jinx tasted him with her own tongue, his thighs hard against hers now. Her blouse came loose from the waistband of her trousers as her arms moved up to curve about his neck, his hair soft and silky to the touch as her fingers caressed his sensitive nape.

His hands slipped under her blouse and felt warm against her bare skin as they moved to touch the arch of her back, moving featherlight across her ribcage before tenderly cupping both her breasts.

Jinx's back arched when Nik's mouth left hers to travel the length of her neck, lingering in the hollows at its base, nibbling erotically on her ear lobes, before licking the sensitive skin below.

His chest was covered in fine dark hairs, Jinx's fingers making their way beneath Nik's shirt and lacing into their silkiness, easily finding the sensitive nubs nestled there. Nik's sharply indrawn groan of breath was evidence of his own pleasure at her searching touch.

Nik unbuttoned and then pushed aside her silky blouse, his mouth moist against the upper curve of her breasts, his hands still cupping, caressing, unerringly finding the fiery tips as he bent to suckle through the lacy material of her bra that was all that separated him from her nakedness.

Heat. Consuming her. The warmth between her thighs was the hottest moist heat imaginable, dragging at her lower limbs with sweet demand, her hands moving to cling to the broad width of his shoulders as she felt weak with need. A need she knew Nik could satisfy, assuage, as no other man could.

His eyes were smoky grey as he raised his head to

look at her searchingly. 'Is this what you want, Jinx?' His voice was husky with his own arousal. 'I hope it is— because I want you very much!' His lips once again sought hers, his kiss lingering, seeking, persuading.

There was no doubting what Nik was asking. No doubting that he wanted her. Or that she wanted him.

But…

It would be so easy to dismiss that *but*, to forget it, if only briefly, and *yet…*

But. And *yet*.

Both expressions of doubt. A doubt that was growing stronger the longer Nik looked at her so compellingly as he waited for her answer.

Entering into a relationship, any relationship, with Nik Prince would be a mistake, Jinx finally accepted painfully, every inch of her protesting as she forced herself to move out of his arms, to turn away to rebutton her blouse with shaking hands.

That task finally completed, she was almost afraid to turn back and look at Nik. She knew that he hadn't moved, could feel the heat of his gaze on her back.

She deliberately walked away from him to stand in front of the window looking down into the busy street below, her back stiffening slightly as she finally heard him move.

But it was only to once again pick up the telephone receiver as he punched out the number with suppressed violence.

Really meant for her? Probably, she accepted huskily. What must a man like Nik think of her, a twenty-eight-year-old woman, too afraid of the physical intimacy they had both craved such a short time ago, because she feared the emotional intimacy that would follow?

'Zak?' he barked into the receiver as his call was obviously answered.

Zak…? His brother, Zak Prince? The legendary golden film star everyone—but especially women!—raved about?

What on earth was the point of Nik telephoning him now, of all times?

'No, I think you have the wrong number,' a distracted voice sounded down the earpiece of the phone.

'Very funny, Zak,' Nik snapped in answer to his younger brother's witty reply, all the time his gaze fixed on Jinx as she stood so aloofly remote in front of the window, the sunshine giving her hair the appearance of living flame. 'Are you in the hotel?' he demanded impatiently of Zak, knowing he was unfairly taking out his foul temper on his brother, but too angry with himself—and Jinx—at that moment to do anything else.

'Uh-oh,' Zak murmured knowingly, obviously giving Nik all of his attention now. 'What—or should I say who?—has upset you, big brother?'

'I'll tell you later,' Nik dismissed—knowing he wouldn't tell Zak any such thing. The fact that he was frustrated as hell, first by Jinx's accusations, and then by her shying off just now, was not something he intended discussing with his little brother. For one thing, it was simply too personal, and for another—Zak probably wouldn't stop laughing for a week at the idea of his big brother being turned down in that way! 'What I need right now is for you to find a beautiful woman—'

'No problem,' Zak assured him. 'Why do you think I'm still in the hotel?' he added mockingly.

Nik would just bet it wasn't a problem for his brother to find a beautiful woman; at thirty-six Zak went through women like other men went through socks! 'Is she single?' he prompted cautiously.

'Of course,' Zak came back slightly indignantly. 'That only happened the once, Nik—and only then because she forgot to mention she was a married woman.'

'Okay,' Nik conceded. 'In that case, I would like the two of you to go down to Reception, making sure you're seen. There's a reporter and photographer waiting down in Reception. I want you to distract them long enough for me to get the hell out of here!' he explained impatiently as Zak would have interrupted.

'Hmm,' Zak mused. 'And can I ask who's going to be leaving with you?'

'No,' Nik snapped.

'And you asked me if I'm with a married woman—'

'Zak!' he warned.

'Okay, okay, give me ten minutes. I'll call you as I'm about to go down. If it rings three times and then stops, that means it's me—'

'Zak, you aren't supposed to be enjoying this!' Nik growled, knowing his brother was doing exactly that—and that he would want some sort of explanation later on today!

'Just give me ten minutes,' Zak told him good-naturedly.

It was probably going to be the longest ten minutes of his life, Nik realized as he slowly put down his receiver, Jinx still turned away from him. Although she couldn't have helped but overhear his half of the telephone conversation, at least.

Not that it would have been much help, he acknowledged ruefully; he wasn't especially known for explaining himself to people, even less so when all he really wanted to do was pull Jinx back into his arms, take her to his bed, and keep her there for a week!

He tensed as she finally turned around, a shutter coming down over his emotions as he took in the paleness of her face, her eyes seeming like huge blue lakes in that paleness. Damn it, she looked like an injured butterfly, all elusive fragility.

'That was very kind of you.' She spoke huskily, her gaze not quite meeting his.

His mouth twisted. 'I've never thought of myself as particularly unkind.'

'I didn't mean—never mind.' The hand she had raised in protest dropped back down to entwine awkwardly with the other one, her expression guarded beneath dark lashes. 'I'm sorry about just now—'

'About what?' Nik tried to sound unconcerned. Damn it, it was bad enough that just one word of encouragement from her and he would be back in her arms, without having her apologize for turning him down!

'It's a woman's prerogative to change her mind, isn't it?' he drawled.

'I was referring to my accusations concerning the reporter, not—' She broke off, sudden warmth colouring her cheeks. 'Never mind,' she mumbled.

No, never mind. The fact that every time he met this woman he was left a frustrated mess was his problem, not hers. It was just that she seemed to get under his skin...

If it weren't for the fact she was J. I. Watson, then he would get the hell away from her—and stay away.

Which, from how she was looking at him, was obviously exactly what she was thinking too!

'Um.' She swallowed hard, almost squirming with discomfort. 'Do you think your brother will be long?'

Of course, she hadn't heard that part of the conversation. 'Ten minutes should do it. Seven now,' he added after a brief glance at his wrist-watch. 'Can I get you a drink while we're waiting?' he offered almost desperately; this was obviously turning out to be the longest ten minutes of his life!

Her tongue moved to moisten her lips, Nik's pulse leaping along with it, although he was pretty sure that Jinx had no idea how provocative the gesture was. There was no way she would have done it if she had!

'A cola, or some other soft drink?' he elaborated as her frown deepened. 'Don't worry, Jinx,' he added scathingly, moving to show her the mini-bar that stood in the corner of the sitting-room, stocked with drinks, nuts and chocolate. 'I have no intention of trying to get you drunk in the middle of the day in order to have my wicked way with you!'

'No,' she confirmed flatly—giving him no idea what she thought of that particular suggestion! 'Does that happen a lot? The thing with the reporter and photographer,' she explained quickly, once again not meeting his gaze.

Just in case he should misunderstand and assume she meant her having turned him down flat!

He grimaced. 'All the time.' He shrugged. 'We all came over a couple of weeks ago for our nephew's christening,' he explained at her questioning look. 'And we've all been avoiding the media ever since,' he added dryly, 'but my little brother Zak, who's still in town because he's discussing his next film with the director, makes much more interesting reading than I do. Talk of the devil,' he said as the telephone began to ring.

Three times before ringing off. As promised.

He really should have a word with his little brother about his knowledge of such subterfuge...

'Right, let's get out of here!' Nik closed the mini-bar, striding over to open the door. 'Jinx?' he prompted as she didn't move; in fact, she seemed rooted to the spot.

She looked at him guardedly. 'You're sure this is going to work?'

No, he wasn't sure this was going to work! Oh, he had no doubts that Zak and his companion would prove a suitable diversion; that wasn't the problem at all. The problem was that he had really annoyed that photographer earlier by taking his camera, and members of the press, once annoyed, tended to stay that way. He also didn't underestimate the intelligence of the reporter or the photographer; Zak arriving downstairs in this way could seem just a little too convenient to one or both of them...

'I'm sure,' he said with more hope than certainty, although there was no way that the reporter could know that Jinx was J. I. Watson. 'Now, once we get downstairs, walk straight through the reception area, don't look left or right, just keep on walking, and then once we're outside we'll get into a taxi and—what?' he rasped as she slowly shook her head, her expression unmistakably sceptical now, the look in her eyes derisive.

'You've done this before, haven't you?' she said knowingly.

'Avoided reporters?' He frowned. 'All the time—'

'No, not that,' Jinx said slowly, no longer looking either apprehensive or remote; in fact, it was difficult to tell how she looked at this moment! 'The telephone call to your brother. The easy way he agreed to help out. The fact that you have some sort of message to let you know he was on his way downstairs.' She indicated the now-silent telephone. 'Nik, just how often have you had to sneak a woman out of your hotel room?'

Now he could tell exactly how she looked—disgusted best described it.

And he wasn't sure whether that emotion was directed at herself or him!

CHAPTER SIX

WHAT a fool she had been!

It was so easy to forget, when Nik held her in his arms, when he kissed her, when he made love to her, exactly what sort of man he was. But the smoothness with which he had dealt with that reporter and photographer earlier, as well as now—with his brother's help, of course!—had very quickly reminded her. Thank goodness!

'Jinx—'

'You have so many things worked out, don't you, Nik?' she scorned. 'The way that you engineered that meeting at Susan and Leo's last weekend, for example. Just how did you know I was going to be there, Nik?' She could tell by the impatient discomfort in his expression that he would rather she hadn't asked that particular question.

'Jinx, you're wasting valuable time—'

'It's my time to waste.' She shrugged.

'And mine—'

'I don't give a damn about your time, Nik—and I'm not leaving here until you answer my question!' Her eyes flashed deeply blue.

He glared at her frustratedly. 'You have to choose *now* to ask me that particular question?'

'Yes!'

He sighed. 'You're not going to like the answer.'

'I didn't think for a moment that I would,' she assured him scathingly. 'I can reason that you were able to write directly to me to organize this morning's meeting, because you discovered the PO box that was used for corresponding with Stephens Publishing—although I have yet to find out who your source was,' she added coldly, deciding it was past time she had words with the publisher. 'But it doesn't follow that that would tell you I would be at Susan and Leo's the weekend before last—Wait a minute! You had me followed from the post office earlier that week when I had lunch with Susan, didn't you?' she realized slowly as Nik looked decidedly uncomfortable now. 'Which means, to know about her anniversary party on Saturday, you must also have had Susan checked out…'

There was no other way he could possibly have found out what her own plans were for that weekend. She had realized his being there at all was too much of a coincidence, but she certainly hadn't realized the lengths to which he had gone—!

'Didn't you?' she breathed incredulously.

'Jinx—'

'You did.' She nodded furiously. 'And my name is Juliet. Or Dr Nixon, if you prefer. Never Jinx as far as you are concerned,' she bit out, grabbing her bag from where she had placed it earlier and walking determinedly to the door. She paused there, turning to glare at him. 'If you—or anyone employed by you,' she added scornfully, 'attempt to come near me again, then that harassment charge I threatened you with last week will become a reality!'

She was so angry that at that moment she could cheerfully have hit him—and felt all the better for it. She simply couldn't believe that anyone could behave in such an underhand way. Or that she could have allowed herself to kiss, and be kissed, by such a man.

He shook his head. 'You're being totally unreasonable—'

'*I'm* being unreasonable?' she hissed. 'Your own behaviour borders on obsessional. Hit a raw nerve, did I?' she spat out as he seemed to pale slightly.

Good, came her inner—childish?—response. But it was about time he knew what it felt like to be on the receiving end for a change. She felt as if she had only just been managing to keep half a step in front of him for the last week and a half—it seemed only fair that she had now decided to turn and challenge him!

What was the old saying—'attack is the best form of defence'…?

Well, where Nik Prince was concerned, attack was the only defence left to her.

'Not at all,' he dismissed stiffly. 'As I pointed out to you last week, such a course of action would only bring about exactly what you're hoping to avoid. Publicity,' he reminded at her questioning look.

Her eyes widened. 'Are you threatening me?'

'Believe it or not, no. No,' he repeated firmly as she continued to look at him sceptically. 'But even if that reporter earlier had no idea who you are, I've made no secret of the fact that I'm looking for J. I. Watson. And if I could find you, then so can someone else.'

Oh, he was unquestionably right about that. Except they weren't talking about 'someone else' at the moment, they were talking about him!

'Let's concentrate on you for the moment, shall we?' Her voice was saccharine-sweet. 'Because if you force me into making this into a legal matter, then I can assure you I will never give you the film rights to *No Ordinary Boy*. In fact,' she added as he would have spoken, 'I'll find out who your biggest rival is and give them to him!'

Nik's gaze narrowed as he looked at her for several long minutes. 'You really would do that, wouldn't you?' he finally said.

At this moment? Angry with herself. Angry with him. Oh, yes, right now she was more than capable of doing something like that.

Tomorrow might be something else entirely…

Although she had no intention of letting the arrogant Nik Prince see that. 'If I'm forced to.' She nodded abruptly.

He drew in a harsh breath. 'Fine. Let's get you out of here, then, shall we? And then—'

'I'm more than capable of getting myself out of here,' she assured him. 'After all, as you've already pointed out, it's you the press are after, not me!'

Although just how long that would last was anybody's guess. Which meant she had some very serious decisions to make during the next couple of days. Decisions she was no nearer making now than she had been a year ago…

'It's only a matter of time, Ji—Juliet,' Nik corrected pointedly as his words echoed her thoughts. 'It was bad enough the first time around, but the mad clamour to find J. I. Watson will start all over again, more intensely, once the second ''Ordinary Boy'' book is published…'

'What do you know about the second ''Boy'' book?' she cut in sharply, every inch of her tensing warily as that icy grey gaze suddenly eluded hers.

Nik made an impatient movement. 'Well, of course there will be a second book—'

'There's no ''of course'' about it,' she said slowly, becoming more sure by the minute that he knew she had already submitted the second manuscript. Just as she was sure that only someone at Stephens Publishing could have told him that...

'Oh, for—' Nik broke off his angry exclamation as the telephone began to ring.

Three times. Just as before. And then ringing off. Just as before.

'Your brother seems to be becoming a little—anxious, at the delay,' Jinx said derisively. 'I suggest you go down and alleviate that anxiety for him.'

'And you?' Nik frowned. 'Where are you going?'

'I don't believe that is any of your business! But I actually intend going out exactly the way I came in— straight out the front door! You're the one they want a story on, Nik—not me. And as far as I'm concerned, they can have you!' she declared before letting herself out of the suite and heading for the lift.

She certainly wasn't going to be part of Nik's story. Either now or in the future. Although she had come very close to becoming exactly that, Jinx realized heavily as the lift descended. She had been so close—too close!— to giving in to the desire he had aroused in her, to just forgetting everything else.

How he would have liked that! Not only would he have managed to find J. I. Watson where everyone else had failed, but he would also believe he had managed to get her into his bed!

Jinx closed her eyes, swaying slightly as she thought of her arousal earlier, her need for the feel of Nik's body against hers, inside hers, loving her, possessing her, until she could think of nothing else.

Had it been only the loneliness of the last eighteen

months, that necessary feeling of distance between her-self and other people, that had caused her intense reaction to Nik? Or had it been something else?

Please let it not be anything else!

Falling in love with a man like Nik Prince, besides being a totally insane thing for her to do, would also be complete anathema to the anonymity of J. I. Watson.

If she needed further proof, the crowd of people gath-ered around Zak Prince and the stunning blonde at his side as Jinx stepped from the lift into the reception area, the reporter of earlier included, was more than enough to convince her of that!

Jinx strode straight through the reception area, outside to where a row of taxis stood waiting, nodding her thanks to the doorman as he opened the back door of the first one for her to get inside. Only starting to breathe easily again once that door had been closed behind her.

'Where to, love?' the driver prompted cheerfully.

'Fold Street, please,' Jinx told him. 'Stephens Publishing on Fold Street,' she repeated firmly before sitting back to stare sightlessly out of the window.

Well, that went well, Nik told himself disgustedly as the door closed decisively behind Jinx, having had no choice but to stand impotently by and watch as she walked out of his life.

Or thought she did.

There was no way, absolutely no way he was letting Jinx just walk away from him like that. Because she was J. I. Watson. Because he still wanted the movie rights to *No Ordinary Boy*.

At least, that was what he told himself. But another

part of him knew that it was because he wanted Jinx Nixon, wanted her in his bed, with no interruptions, for as long as it took to sate both himself and her. Maybe then he would be able to get her out of his head, out of the dreams he had been having about her this last week, naked and willing as he made love to her in every imaginative way he could think of.

He had never allowed a woman to get between him and his work. And Jinx Nixon was going to be no exception.

'What the hell happened to you?' Zak demanded a few minutes later as Nik opened the door to let him into his suite. 'I kept the press busy for as long as I possibly could—much to Damson Grey's delight. Yes, that is who spent the night with me.' Zak grinned at Nik's disgusted snort. 'And, believe me, her body more than lives up to her name!' His grin widened as he threw himself down into one of the armchairs to look up at Nik.

He was one of the scruffiest men Nik had ever seen, both on and off the screen. It never ceased to amaze Nik how his brother drew women to him like a magnet. Of course, it could have something to do with Zak's golden good looks: overlong blond hair, laughing blue eyes set in a face so handsome he was almost beautiful, his body long and loose-limbed in the faded denims and baggy black tee shirt.

'So where is she?' Zak prompted as he looked conspiratorially around the suite. 'Still hiding in the bedroom?'

To Nik's self-disgust, he found himself tensing resentfully at this offhand remark directed at Jinx. 'She was never in the bedroom,' he bit out reprovingly.

'She wasn't?' Zak's eyes widened speculatively. 'So where is she now?' he asked before Nik could give him another cutting reply.

'I have no idea,' Nik answered him honestly. 'She walked out of here about five minutes ago. In fact, you may have seen her on her way out.' He frowned as the thought occurred to him.

Zak gave the idea some thought, his brow clearing suddenly. 'Tiny little thing? Long red hair, very deep blue eyes? A very kissable—'

'That's enough!' Nik growled.

Zak's eyes widened. 'Yep, I guess that was the one,' he teased. 'And you never made it as far as the bedroom? Maybe that's why you're in such a foul mood, big brother. Self-denial isn't good for a man of your advanced years!'

Zak could say that again! Not the part about his advanced years, of course, but this constant frustration certainly wasn't doing anything for his mood.

Although Nik's discomfort was nothing compared to his concern now for Jinx and what she would do next. Because he didn't doubt that she intended doing something.

'Will you excuse me, Zak?' he murmured distractedly. 'I have to go out for a while.' He picked up his brown leather jacket and pulled it on over his shirt, checking in his trouser pockets for his wallet.

'Going after the beautiful—what is her name?' Zak queried.

'Her name is Juliet. And stay away from her, little brother. Well away.' He scowled darkly.

Zak's grin was wider than ever. 'Wow, this is a first!

Can I use your phone? I have to ring Rik at Stazy's and tell him—'

'Use your own phone,' Nik snapped. 'And tell Rik what, exactly?'

'That our BB has been bowled over by a five-foot nothing of a woman with the body of Venus, of course.' Zak stood up, heading for the bar, taking out a cola and drinking it straight from the bottle.

'Help yourself!' Nik drawled, giving an impatient shake of his head. 'And I would hold off telling Rik anything, if I were you,' he added as he headed for the door. 'Things aren't always what they seem, Zak.'

His brother frowned meditatively. 'Now you've really got me curious…!'

That wasn't quite the idea; the last thing Nik needed right now was Zak and Rik on his case. He was confused enough about Jinx as it was!

'Feel like telling me where you're going?' Zak quirked mocking brows.

'Nope.'

Zak shrugged. 'Maybe I'll catch up with you later.'

'Maybe,' he echoed, frowning heavily as he left the hotel suite.

Where would Jinx have gone after she left him? Home? Or somewhere else? Bearing in mind how angry she had been when she'd left, he had a feeling it wasn't the former. If he were in Jinx's shoes, he'd go—

'Fold Street,' he told the taxi driver as he got in the back of the black vehicle. 'Stephens Publishing,' he added tersely.

The journey seemed interminable, the taxi meeting every conceivable hold-up possible, from someone falling off their bicycle to a set of failed traffic lights. All of which only served to increase Nik's impatience to boiling point.

Jinx had been in a furious mood when she'd left—because of him, admittedly, but he had a definite feeling that anger might spill over onto whomever she spoke to next. If his guess was correct, and Jinx had gone to Stephens Publishing, then, after months of never even meeting his author, James wasn't going to know what hit him!

Maybe they would be lucky and James would be out of the office!

No such luck, Nik groaned inwardly after the receptionist had called James Stephens's secretary and okayed him to go up.

Maybe he was wrong, after all, Nik reasoned on the way up in the lift; the secretary would hardly have allowed him up if there were a full-scale battle going on in James's office.

In which case, he had better do some quick thinking as to what he was doing here!

'You can go right in,' James's secretary looked up to tell him smilingly as he strode into the office.

Great; besides feeling rather foolish for having rushed over here in order to save Jinx from herself by telling James Stephens exactly what she thought of him and his publishing company, Nik was also no nearer to knowing what to tell the other man about his own reason for being here!

'Come in, Nik,' James welcomed him brightly, having stood up to come round his desk and shake Nik by the hand, effectively blocking Nik's view of the rest of the office so he couldn't see whether or not Jinx was actually here.

James smiled at him warmly. 'How fortunate that you should arrive just now.' He beamed. 'You're not going to believe this, but I can actually introduce you to our author J. I. Watson at last!' He finally stepped to one side, leaving Nik with a clear view of Jinx as she sat in the chair facing the other man's desk.

She was sitting sideways in the chair at the moment, that clear violet-blue gaze coldly mocking as she looked up at him challengingly.

Affording Nik little pleasure in knowing he had been right in his surmise as to where she had gone after leaving him…!

CHAPTER SEVEN

'MR PRINCE.' Jinx nodded to him coolly, exerting every ounce of will-power she possessed to remain calmly seated, when every instinct she had screamed for her to stand up defensively as Nik looked down at her with narrowed grey eyes.

The fact that he was here at all was enough to set her nerve endings jangling—even though she'd had prior warning of his imminent arrival when James Stephens's secretary had called through a couple of minutes ago.

But the question was, why was Nik here?

Had he followed her here? Or had he come for reasons of his own?

More to the point, was he going to acknowledge that the two of them already knew each other?

She had arrived here earlier with the sole purpose of telling James Stephens exactly what she thought of his publishing company before demanding her second manuscript back, but the publisher had been so pleased and excited to meet her at last, so obviously genuine in his pleasure, like a little boy who had been given an early Christmas present, that she simply hadn't had the heart to say all those unpleasant things to this genially friendly man.

'Miss Nixon,' Nik greeted her abruptly.

'Can you believe that J. I. Watson has been a woman all this time?' James murmured incredulously as he moved to sit back behind his desk.

'Miss Nixon and I have already met, actually,' Nik admitted.

'You have?' James Stephens looked disappointed as he glanced first at Nik and then back to Jinx.

'Only briefly.' Jinx was the one to expand on that statement. 'But long enough for me to inform Mr Prince that I have no intention of giving him the film rights to *No Ordinary Boy*,' she added tightly.

'Ah,' James breathed softly, grimacing his disappointment.

Jinx's eyes widened. 'I take it that you are in favour of Mr Prince making the film?'

The publisher looked uncomfortable now, obviously debating which of them he should offend—because he had to be aware that whichever way he answered he was going to offend one of them!

He seemed to choose his words carefully. 'If the film were to be made, then I have to say I couldn't think of a finer director than Nik here!'

Jinx had to smile inwardly at the man's tact. 'But the film isn't going to be made,' she said firmly, 'so whether or not Mr Prince is a fine director or not is totally irrelevant.' She raised mocking brows as Nik's mouth tightened grimly at the ambiguity of her remark.

Deliberately so. She knew he was a brilliant director; the whole world knew he was a brilliant director; she just had no intention of adding to his fan club by admitting as much!

'Yes,' James Stephens accepted slowly. 'I—' He broke off as the internal telephone rang on his desk. 'Excuse me.' He smiled apologetically before taking the call.

Probably relieved to get a few moments' respite from the building tension he could sense around him, Jinx guessed ruefully. She—

'What are you doing here?' Nik murmured in a force-ful undertone.

Her eyes widened. 'I have a perfect right to visit my publisher if I so wish,' she told him coldly.

'But you never have before.'

'And I probably never will again!' Jinx stood up rest-lessly, moving across the room to stare out of the win-dow, sensing Nik's presence inches behind her as he fol-lowed her. 'What are *you* doing here?' she demanded insultingly.

'Believe it or not, saving you from yourself,' he came back dryly.

She turned to look at him with wide eyes. 'I beg your pardon?'

Nik grimaced. 'You were in a reckless mood when you left the hotel earlier—'

'I wonder why that was!' she snapped.

'Jinx—' He had reached out to touch her, but held his hand up defensively as she flinched away from him. 'Juliet,' he bit out tautly. 'I didn't want you to do some-thing…impulsive, where James was concerned, when it's me you're really mad at!'

He was right, of course, she had come here intending to tell James Stephens that one of his many employees couldn't be trusted, before demanding the second man-uscript back.

Because she was mad at Nik.

And herself…

But she would think about that later, when she was alone, not here and now, when Nik was much too close for comfort.

'I'm not mad at you, Nik. I don't know you well enough to be mad at you,' she said insultingly.

His face darkened. 'That isn't true, and you know it—'

'Sorry about that,' James Stephens apologized as he concluded his call. 'Coincidentally, that was your editor, Miss Nixon. I've told her that you and Mr Prince are here, and asked her to join us.'

Jinx hadn't come here with the idea of her visit turning into a social event! In fact, she regretted coming here at all now…

But once again James Stephens looked so pleased with himself and the way things were turning out that Jinx didn't have the heart to disappoint him.

'I'm afraid I can only stay a few more minutes; I have a previous engagement for lunch.' She smiled to take the sting out of her words.

'I was hoping you might let me take you out to lunch.' James frowned. 'Having met you at last, I really don't want to lose you again so quickly,' he added charmingly.

Jinx avoided looking at Nik as he gave a sceptical snort. 'Another time, perhaps.' She was deliberately vague, having no intention of there ever being 'another time'.

She should never have come here, never have blown her anonymity in this way. It was Nik Prince's fault that she had done so. He—

'Ah, Jane.' James Stephens stood up as a tall blonde woman entered his office after the briefest of knocks. 'I want you to meet our author, J. I. Watson,' he announced triumphantly as he moved forward to lightly grasp Jinx's arm.

As if afraid she might try to escape, or at the very least evaporate in front of his eyes, if he didn't hold onto her!

The beautiful blonde Jinx could now identify as her editor, Jane Morrow, moved forward to shake Jinx by the hand, although her smile was bland as she turned to look at Nik.

But it was Nik's response to the other woman's presence in the room that caught and held Jinx's attention; she was able to feel his tension as he looked at the other woman guardedly. A tension he did his best to hide as he seemed to sense Jinx's interest, giving her a tight smile before turning to gaze out of the window at the London skyline.

A view Jinx was almost certain he didn't even see!

She gave her editor a closer look, noting the smooth beauty of the other woman's face, her slender curves in the black business suit she wore, her fingers bare of rings, her legs long and shapely. Attractive enough for Nik Prince to have used his practised charm upon?

The other woman's smile warmed as she turned back to Jinx, blue eyes glowing with enthusiasm. 'It's such a pleasure to meet you at last!' she gushed.

No, Jinx decided, the arrogant Nik Prince wouldn't find this gushing, clinging woman in the least attractive. So what had been the reason for his tension when the other woman had come into the room? Surely Jane Morrow, her own editor, couldn't be the one to have leaked information concerning her identity? That just didn't make sense. But, then, what did make sense about any of this situation she now found herself in?

'Thank you,' she accepted lightly. 'I was actually just telling James that I have to go now.' That she should never have come here in the first place!

'Surely not?' Jane Morrow frowned her disappointment. 'We have so much to talk about, so many questions I would like to ask you. The second manuscript is wonderful, by the way,' she added delightedly. 'So many second books aren't, you know, that…'

Jinx tuned out the other woman's praise, instead turning to look curiously at Nik as she once again sensed the tension in his rigidly straight back.

'It's so kind of you to say so—' Jinx nodded to Jane Morrow as the other woman paused to draw breath '—but I really do have to get going.'

'But you will come back?' Jane Morrow asked.

She swallowed hard as both Jane Morrow and James Stephens looked at her expectantly. They were both nice people, Jinx accepted that, not at all the hard-bitten monsters of the publishing world that she had imagined, and certainly neither of them could be the 'mole' she had told James about before Nik's untimely arrival. But, nice as they were, Jinx knew she had no intention of repeating today's visit...

She moistened dry lips as she formed a polite refusal in her mind. 'I don't really think—'

'I think Miss Nixon is slightly overwhelmed,' Nik was the one to cut in firmly as he turned away from that sightless contemplation out the window. 'Maybe it might be better to let her contact you, James, when she feels up to another visit?'

If it weren't for the fact that he made her sound like a simple-minded idiot scared of her own shadow, Jinx might have felt grateful for Nik's intervention. As it was, he made her feel like a nervous spinster thrown into total confusion by having so much attention paid to her!

'I think, Mr Prince,' she bit out tartly, 'that I am more than capable of deciding that for myself, thank you very much!'

He raised dark brows impatiently before giving a dismissive shrug. 'Fine,' he grated, once again turning away.

She turned back to James Stephens. 'I—I'll call you, shall I?'

The publisher didn't look at all happy with this idea, but one look at the determination on her face seemed to tell him that it was the best he was going to get.

'Fine,' he said regretfully. 'And I will look into that other matter we discussed,' he added.

'Good,' Jinx replied.

'What other matter?' Nik queried.

Jinx shot him a resentful glare. 'Nothing that concerns you, I can assure you, Mr Prince.'

James Stephens once again took her hand in his. 'In the meantime, please feel free to drop in again any time,' he encouraged warmly. 'Let me take you out to lunch next time. Jane, too, of course.'

'Lovely,' Jinx answered noncommittally. 'It was nice to meet you, Miss Morrow,' she added in parting to the other woman, deliberately not so much as glancing in Nik's direction as she hurried out of the office.

As if the hounds of hell were at her heels!

And she didn't relax again until she was seated in the back of yet another taxi taking her home, resting her head back against the seat, her eyes closed, almost able to hear the rapid pounding of her heart.

Never again!

Never again would she allow her emotions to rule her head in that way. She knew what she had to do, knew the dangers attached to revealing the identity of J. I. Watson. And today she had almost blown that.

Because of Nik Prince.

Because he had made her angry.

Because, against all the odds, she knew she was falling in love with him…!

'Well, well, well,' Jane Morrow drawled as she and Nik left James Stephens's office together. 'Who would have thought that J. I. Watson would turn out to be a woman?'

'Yes,' he returned neutrally, anxious to be gone. If he hurried he might still be able to catch up with Jinx before she left. He knew without a doubt that it would be his only chance of finding her again! Whatever had driven her to come here at all—and he had a distinct feeling it was anger towards him!—he knew, even if James Stephens didn't, that she would never come here again.

Jane quirked teasing brows at him. 'Makes your life a lot easier, though, doesn't it?'

'Sorry?' Nik deliberately kept his expression bland, having no idea yet where this conversation was going. Having little interest, either, if he was honest.

'Oh, come on, Nik.' Jane laughed huskily as she touched him lightly on the chest. 'You know how good you are at charming women.'

His mouth tightened, even while he inwardly acknowledged that he probably deserved that remark from this woman. He had set out to charm her, although, to be fair, Jane had given every indication that she wanted to be charmed!

'Possibly. If you'll excuse me, Jane? I'm afraid I have to meet someone.' He knew he probably sounded rude, but he was very conscious of the precious seconds ticking away on the clock.

'Of course.' She slowly removed her hand from his chest, blue eyes hard now. 'You know where I am if you feel like company.'

She knew where he was too, but the likelihood of either of them actually contacting the other was extremely remote.

Although that wasn't to say Nik wasn't completely conscious of her glacial gaze on him all the time he walked down the carpeted corridor to the lift, that feeling confirmed as he turned once inside the lift and saw her still standing exactly where he had left her. She raised a mocking hand in parting, and Nik was relieved when the lift doors closed and shut out her image. After the way they had parted last time, he had been a little surprised by her initial friendliness, although it hadn't taken too long for her to revert back to derisive anger at his obvious lack of interest.

Not very gallant of him, he accepted, but, for some reason he couldn't completely explain, Jane Morrow's hand on his chest just now had given him a distinct feeling of distaste.

It couldn't be because he was falling for Jinx, could it? a little voice mocked inside his head. A little voice that sounded decidedly like Zak's voice teasing him!

And the answer was…no, he wasn't falling for Jinx. She seemed extremely vulnerable to him, very much alone, which probably brought out the same protective instinct in him that he felt towards his sister Stazy, but he certainly *wasn't* falling for her.

Protesting too much, BB?

Zak's voice again, damn it. And he had told both Zak and Rik repeatedly not to call him Big Brother.

But then, if he wasn't falling for Jinx, exactly what was he doing chasing all over London after her in cabs?

Securing the movie rights to a book, that was what!

Lame, Nik, extremely lame. He might as well admit it, to himself if to no one else: the movie had become secondary in his pursuit of Jinx. She was what he wanted right now, every satiny inch of her naked beneath him, her legs wrapped about his hips as they took each other to the heights and back.

He was so lost in thoughts of that image as he came

out of the building onto the pavement that he almost missed Jinx's cab pulling away from the kerb. Mentally cursing himself for his daydreaming, he rushed forward to hail another cab, climbing inside to tell the driver to follow the cab ahead.

The sideways glance he received from the cabbie in the overhead driving mirror, even as he turned the vehicle out into the flow of traffic, was enough to make Nik feel like a character in a second-rate movie. And he had never made a second-rate movie in his life, let alone starred in one.

'The lady left her purse behind,' he leant forward to mutter.

He received another sideways glance for his trouble. 'Course she did, mate!' the cabbie said skeptically.

Nik decided to ignore the driver and instead concentrate on the cab ahead. He could just see Jinx's head above the back seat, that fiery red hair unmistakable. She wasn't going to like the fact that he was following her, so he would have to make sure—

'I 'ate to say this, guv'ner,' the cabbie cut in on his thoughts a few minutes later, 'but I 'ave a feeling that someone's following you too. The taxi be'ind is sticking pretty close, if ya know what I mean?'

Nik did know what he meant, having glanced back to see another black cab almost driving on the bumper of this one, two passengers visible in the back of the vehicle, even if their features were indistinguishable. But every turn that this cab took as it followed behind Jinx, the one behind followed.

Reporters again? Nik couldn't think of anyone else it could be. And if it was the same two from earlier this morning, they were obviously ticked off with him enough to be dogged in their pursuit.

'Can you lose them?' he asked his driver.

'I can try,' the man came back with a cheeky grin, obviously relishing the thought. 'But I might lose sight of the cab in front if I do that.'

Continue to follow Jinx? Or lose the cab behind?

After this morning's fiasco, Jinx certainly wasn't going to thank him if he should lead a reporter directly to her door. But if he had the driver divert from following her, in an effort to divert the cab following his, Nik had a feeling he might never find Jinx again.

Something that didn't please him at all.

Neither choice was a good one as far as he was concerned.

'Okay,' he sighed heavily. 'Turn off at the end of the next block and let's lose these guys.' And he would lose Jinx…

He gazed regretfully after her cab as his driver took the next left turn, her own cab continuing straight on.

'Uh oh,' his driver murmured a few seconds later.

'What is it?' Nik demanded sharply.

The man shrugged. 'Guess they weren't following you, after all.'

'What do you mean?'

'Take a look.' The man grimaced.

Nik turned to look out the back window, the other cab no longer in sight. 'Where did they go?'

Surely they couldn't both have been wrong, after all? If they had, and the cab just happened to have been going the same way that they were, that meant he had lost Jinx for absolutely no reason.

'They continued to follow the other cab, I'm afraid, guv,' the man told him apologetically.

Nik frowned at the empty road behind them. 'Are you sure?'

'Positive.'

Nik didn't hesitate. 'Turn back onto the other road, will you, and see if you can catch them up again?'

While he tried to work out exactly what was going on!

He had assumed, both he and Jinx—after a little persuasion on his part—that the reporter from this morning was following him in the hopes of getting a story, that Jinx's presence there just happened to be coincidental. But what if they had both been wrong…?

Now that he thought about it, he remembered that the woman who had turned out to be a reporter had already been in the hotel when he'd met Jinx in Reception this morning, sitting in one of the chairs there apparently reading a newspaper.

She had then followed them through to the lounge, again seemingly reading a newspaper as she drank a cup of coffee.

But what if following Nik was only a means to an end, in the hopes that he'd lead the reporter and her photographer to the mysterious author J. I. Watson…?

Something he had undoubtedly done!

CHAPTER EIGHT

JINX heaved a sigh of relief as the taxi pulled in next to the kerb beside her home, so weary now that she didn't even want to think about—

'Get out of the cab and go into the house, Jinx! Quickly!' Nik Prince instructed grimly as he wrenched open the door beside her.

She stared up at him dazedly. Where on earth had he come from? More to the point, how had he got here? If he had been following her again—

'I don't have time to explain now, Jinx,' he muttered impatiently, starting to pull her out of the taxi. 'Just go inside and lock the door!'

She blinked up at him incredulously as she suddenly found herself out on the pavement beside him. 'Now just listen here, Nik—'

'Now, Jinx!' he rasped, taking her firmly by the shoulders and turning her in the direction of the house.

One glance at the reporter from this morning, the photographer at her side—obviously with a replacement film if the fact that he was focusing the machine on her was any indication—as the two of them hurried across the pavement towards her was enough to send Jinx hurtling in the direction of the house as if the devil were at her heels.

She almost dropped her door key in her hurry to unlock the door, shooting one last frantic glance in Nik's direction as he stood arguing with the reporter and photographer, before she escaped into the house and closed the door firmly behind her.

Only to lean weakly back against it, breathing heavily, the pounding of her heart sounding loudly in the hallway.

She had thought—hoped!—that things couldn't get any worse after this morning, but this was worse, so much worse, than anything she could have imagined!

Her home, the privacy she so valued, was now completely violated.

They would have to move again, she realized, get completely away from here. There was no way—

A loud pounding sounded on the door behind her. 'Open the damned door, Jinx! Now!' Nik ordered.

As if he had any right to tell her to do anything! As if—

'For God's sake, Jinx!' He rapped loudly on the door again.

She didn't want to let him in. Didn't want his presence in her home. Didn't want to remember his ever having been here. Didn't—

'I know you're there, Jinx—' his voice was menacingly soft now '—so just let me in and we can talk about this.'

Talk? What was there to talk about? Not only had he followed her here, but he had brought a reporter with him.

'Unless you would rather just leave me alone out here with this reporter?'

Her fingers fumbled with the lock as she turned the knob, suddenly finding herself pushed to one side as the door immediately sprang open and Nik forced his way inside, slamming the door behind him.

Jinx just stared at him, her eyes accusing, her face pale.

'Don't look at me like that!' he growled, closing his

eyes briefly before raising his lids to look at her with glittering grey eyes. 'No matter what you may think, I am not responsible for—for that!' he told her grimly, moving restlessly away from the door.

Jinx took a step backwards, effectively blocking the hallway, as if to stop him going any further inside. She couldn't help herself, the move purely instinctive.

'Jinx…!' Nik groaned almost pleadingly.

'You—' She broke off as a knock sounded on the door behind him, her expression scathing now. 'Shouldn't you answer that?'

His eyes glittered angrily. 'Don't make this any worse than it already is, Jinx—'

'Is that possible?' she snapped, wondering how this nightmare was going to end.

Not only did Nik Prince know where she lived, but a reporter did too!

'Probably not,' he conceded. 'But, I repeat, I am not responsible for bringing that reporter here.'

Of course he was responsible; she certainly hadn't invited a reporter to her home. If Nik hadn't followed her—

'Why did you follow me?' she accused.

He looked uncomfortable now. 'You know why,' he muttered.

Oh, yes, she knew why; Nik had been all too aware that once she left James Stephens's office none of them—but Nik especially!—would ever see her again.

She shook her head. 'You've only made this so much worse, Nik. Are they ever going to go away?' She groaned as the knock sounded on the door once again.

'Not for a while, at least.' He grimaced, taking a firm hold of her arm. 'Let's go somewhere where we can't hear them—'

'Let's not,' Jinx contradicted, pointedly removing her arm from the hold he had of her. 'Do you think they managed to get a photograph?' She frowned at the thought.

He winced. 'Maybe not…'

'In other words—yes,' Jinx sighed. 'This is such a mess. I don't know what to do next. I—' She broke off as the door opened at the end of the hallway.

'Juliet, is that you, dear?'

She pushed past Nik, smiling brightly as she walked down the hallway to meet her father. He was a tall, spare man, iron-grey hair brushed neatly back, dressed in his familiar tweed suit and checked shirt, but the whole effect was slightly marred by the carpet slippers he was wearing with them. 'Yes, it's me, Daddy,' she confirmed gently. 'Where is Mrs Holt?'

Her father looked slightly vague. 'In the kitchen preparing lunch, I think. I—there appears to be someone at the door.' A frown furrowed his brow as another knock sounded on the door. 'I—that was quick.' He smiled enquiringly as he spotted Nik standing just in front of the closed door. 'How do you do, young man?' He moved forward to hold out his hand to Nik. 'I'm Jack Nixon.'

Jinx was dismayed. Nik was an intelligent as well as astute man, and it wouldn't take him too long to realize in exactly what way her father 'wasn't well'…

'Nik Prince, sir,' Nik returned respectfully as he shook the other man's hand, a good thirty years younger than Jinx's father. 'I hope we're not disturbing you?'

'Not at all,' the older man assured him. 'We get so few visitors nowadays,' he added wistfully. 'Perhaps you would like to stay to lunch? I believe Mrs Holt said it's chicken salad. I like chicken salad. Do you like chicken salad, young man?'

Jinx felt her heart contract at her father's childish pleasure in such a small thing as having chicken salad for lunch, her gaze instantly becoming guarded as Nik turned to her with a frown.

'Mr Prince isn't staying to lunch, Daddy,' she was the one to answer quickly. 'In fact, I believe he was just on his way…?' She gave him a pointed glare.

Nik's expression was deliberately bland. 'I'm not in any particular hurry,' he said slowly.

'Good. Good.' Jinx's father beamed, his blue eyes pale and watery now, lacking the sharp intelligence they had once had. 'I'll just go and tell Mrs Holt that there's one extra for lunch.' He shuffled off in the slightly overlarge carpet slippers.

Silence followed his departure. Jinx was loath to look up at Nik and see the questioning look she was sure would be on his face, and Nik remained quietly patient as he waited for her to say something.

But what could she say? Excuse my father, but he isn't quite himself nowadays?

Not quite himself! Her father had once been one of the foremost experts on Jacobite history in this country, had taught the subject for over forty years, was consulted by other learned minds as to his opinion on certain events.

But that had been once…

Nowadays her father seemed to have trouble remembering what day it was, let alone what year, and if he still had his knowledge of history then it was buried somewhere behind the vagueness of his expression.

But how could she say any of that without having Nik feel sorry for her father?

Because she didn't want Nik to pity her father. Didn't want anyone to pity him, when he had once been a man so respected and revered by his peers.

'Jinx…?'

Her head rose defensively as she finally looked up at Nik, her gaze challenging him to say anything that could be interpreted as pitying or—worse!—condescending.

Whatever he said next had to be the right thing, Nik knew, or Jinx would cast him from her life and never see him again. And that, he realized, was totally unacceptable to him.

Because of the movie he wanted to make of *No Ordinary Boy*?

The movie didn't even come into it! In fact, if he was honest, it hadn't been a factor for some time now. Jinx was what mattered. And at this moment, the reporter outside apart, he was walking on very shaky ground where she was concerned…

'What happened?' he asked gently.

'What makes you think something happened?' If anything her chin rose even higher.

But unless Nik was mistaken, the new brightness to her eyes was due to unshed tears and not the anger of a few minutes ago. 'I—your father—' He drew in a deep breath, very aware of that knife edge he was balanced upon. 'Did he have a breakdown of some kind?' He decided briskness was probably the way to go; pity he knew Jinx would totally reject, gentleness probably the same.

'Of some kind,' she admitted, every inch of her seeming to be covered in defensive prickles. 'What are we going to do about the reporter and photographer outside?' she abruptly changed the subject.

Nik shrugged. 'Have lunch with your father, and then see if they're still there?' He was pushing it, he knew, but he really did want to find out more about this situation than he knew now.

Although just seeing Jinx's father answered a lot of questions for him. There was no way that Jack Nixon could withstand the sort of publicity that would prevail if it were known that his daughter was the author of *No Ordinary Boy*. The press could be dogged, intrusive, stripping one's life down to the bare bones, and still carry on looking for more. Nik had no doubts that Jack Nixon's delicate mental health wouldn't be able to cope with something like that.

Something he was sure Jinx was all too aware of, too...

'I have a better suggestion,' she came back tartly now. 'You leave, taking the reporter and photographer with you, and I'll go and have lunch with my father!'

Nik grimaced, having expected her to say something like that. And on the face of it, it must seem like the practical thing to do. Except that it had been Jinx the reporter and photographer had been following.

Which meant they must have some idea that she was the author J. I. Watson.

As far as he was aware only three people, possibly four, knew that Jinx was the author J. I. Watson: himself, Jane Morrow, James Stephens, and possibly James Stephens's secretary, none of whom benefited in any way by revealing that information to the press.

But, nevertheless, Nik was sure that the information had leaked out somehow.

He just wasn't sure it was a good idea to tell Jinx that just yet. She was already as jumpy as a cat, and furiously angry with him. If she thought that he was somehow responsible—!

He smiled. 'I think I like my plan better.'

Her cheeks flushed angrily. 'Well, that's too bad, be-cause—'

'Lunch is ready!' Jinx's father came back into the hallway to announce brightly.

Nik's gaze narrowed thoughtfully as it rested on the other man. Jinx hadn't answered his question earlier concerning what had happened to make her father like this. Because he was pretty sure that something had. Something of a highly emotional nature.

Something that had affected Jinx, too…?

He wasn't sure yet. But he definitely wanted to find out.

Which was extraordinary in itself, he admitted wryly. Most people would call his single-mindedness where his work was concerned arrogant, but he preferred to think of it as being focused. Maybe that was an arrogance in itself? Probably, but it was the way he worked. One thing at a time, everything compartmentalized.

But Jinx, with her fiery hair, violet-blue eyes, and a body that answered his, made a nonsense of that compartmentalization, causing everything that was important to him at this moment to overlap itself; the movie of *No Ordinary Boy*, the puzzle of Jackson Nixon, but, most of all, Jinx herself.

She interested him more than any of those other things!

'Lunch is ready,' he told her.

She shot him an impatient glance, but was obviously very aware of her father waiting for them at the end of the hallway.

'Jinx…?' Nik prompted.

'Fine,' she snapped. 'But you and I will definitely talk later,' she muttered so that only he could hear.

There were much pleasanter things he could think of to do with Jinx than talking, but if that was all that was on offer at the moment—and he was pretty sure that it was!—then he would take what he could get.

'I'll look forward to it,' he assured her huskily, raising innocent brows as she looked up at him with brief suspicion before following her father through to the back of the house.

The three of them had lunch outside sitting at a table under a sun umbrella in the well-maintained back garden—a garden that was, thankfully, completely closed in by a six-foot-high fence. Nik knew better than most exactly how tenacious reporters could be once on the scent of a story—they were quite capable of looking through windows and over fences in order to get what they wanted. And they obviously hadn't given up on Jinx yet...

Despite the fact that Jinx obviously wished him well away from here, that her father's conversation lacked the intelligence he was so well known for, Nik enjoyed the next hour spent in their company.

He saw a gentler side of Jinx as she conversed with her father, that gentleness obviously a calming influence on the older man as he took childish pleasure in her company. Not that Nik had ever found Jinx to be an aggressive person; it was just that she was usually so on the defensive when he was around that this softer side was a revelation to him.

Everything about Juliet India Nixon was a revelation to him, the attraction he felt towards her like nothing he had ever felt before. And it seemed to be getting more intense the longer he was around her, rather than diminishing as it usually did when he spent too much time in one woman's company.

He loved to watch the elegance of her slender hands as she ate, or pushed the coppery swathe of her hair back from her cheeks. The gentle curves of her body, curves he longed to touch. The way a little dimple appeared in one cheek when she smiled at her father—not at Nik, because she hadn't smiled at him once all the way through the meal!

Not that her father seemed to have noticed any strain between Jinx and Nik, just enjoying their company completely oblivious of the tension between them.

'Time for your nap, Daddy,' Jinx told her father as Mrs Holt came to clear away the remains of the meal.

Jack Nixon rose slowly to his feet. 'Never get old, Nik,' he warned ruefully even as he followed the housekeeper back into the house. 'The man becomes the child again!'

Nik's gaze was speculative as he watched the other man enter the house. That last comment had been quite an intelligent observation for a man who seemed totally unaware of his surroundings most of the time, let alone anything else.

'There are the occasional flashes of—of his old self, shall we say?' Jinx said, obviously having watched Nik watching her father. 'But unfortunately they don't usually last for long,' she added sadly.

Nik frowned; Jinx was too beautiful, too lovely a person, to be sad. Surely something could be done…? 'Has he seen anyone? A specialist, something like that?' he asked—and as quickly wished that he hadn't as Jinx stiffened resentfully.

'He had several months in a nursing home, after the initial shock,' she finally answered distantly. 'But, quite honestly, it did no good. He's better off at home, anyway.'

Nik nodded. 'Mrs Holt watches out for him when you have to go out?'

'Yes. Nik, I really think that you should go now. The

reporter and her friend have probably given up by now and gone home—'

'Doubtful,' he dismissed from experience. 'What was the "initial shock", Jinx?' he queried astutely, knowing by the way she became even more coldly aloof that he had touched on a subject she would rather not talk about.

But if he were to help either of these people—and he really thought that he must—he had to know what trauma Jackson Nixon had suffered.

The same trauma that had also helped to create the fiercely private woman Jinx was now…?

CHAPTER NINE

JINX stared at him, unsure of what to say in answer to that particular question. On the one hand, the less Nik Prince knew about her or her family, the better she was sure it would be. But if she stood any chance of making him go away—and staying away!—then she knew she had to at least tell him some of what had happened eighteen months ago.

She drew in a ragged breath. 'Come through to my father's study with me—oh, yes, he has a study,' she confirmed heavily as Nik raised surprised brows. 'Not that he's ever used this one.' She sighed. 'But I still brought everything with me when we moved six months ago.'

Just in case, she had been telling herself this last eighteen months. Just in case her father made some sort of miraculous recovery and decided to finish the book on the Jacobite uprising that he had been working on when— When—

'This way.' She led the way further down the hallway, opening the door at the end and ushering Nik inside.

'Study' was probably rather a complimentary way of describing the room that they entered. The shelved walls, and most of the floor space, were covered in books, both for reading and reference, and the desk was awash with papers and framed photographs.

It was one of the latter that Jinx picked up and handed to Nik, at the same time keeping her gaze deliberately averted from his.

She knew exactly what he would see in the photograph: a family sitting on a blanket eating a picnic beside a river, all of them smiling happily into the camera.

Her mother. Her father. Her brother. Herself.

Just a normal family snapshot.

Except that it wasn't the whole picture…

'Where are your mother and brother now?' Nik asked with that astuteness Jinx had come to expect of him.

'They died eighteen months ago,' she answered flatly. 'In case you're interested, my mother's maiden name was Watson,' she added dryly.

Nik continued to look at her, his stillness letting her know he expected her to add something to that remark. But what could she say? Her mother and Jamie were both dead. There was nothing else to say.

'The shock was too much for my father,' she added abruptly when she couldn't stand that expectant silence a moment longer. 'I—he's been like this—' she raised her hands helplessly '—ever since.'

Nik gave the photograph another long look before replacing it back on the desktop. 'Wasn't that just a little selfish of him? After all, it wasn't just his wife and son who died, but your mother and brother too.'

'You don't understand!' Jinx snapped, deeply resentful of this criticism of her father. 'You know nothing about the situation at all, Nik, so how dare you come here and presume to sit in judgement—?'

'Calm down, Jinx,' Nik soothed. 'I was only—'

'I know what you *were only*,' she accused. 'I think it's time you left now.' She turned away. 'Past time!'

She had been stupid to have ever hoped for Nik's understanding; after all, his only interest in her was the film rights to *No Ordinary Boy*. Something she kept forgetting!

Because every time she was around him all she could think about was how attracted she was to him. It was there all the time, a thrum of awareness beneath her skin. As for what had happened between them at his hotel earlier…!

'I want you to leave, Nik,' she repeated.

'Do you?'

When had he got so close? At what point in their conversation had he moved so that he was now standing only inches away from her? Causing that thrumming sensation beneath her skin to increase so that every inch of her was tinglingly alive!

She moistened dry lips. 'Yes. I—'

'I don't think so, Jinx,' he murmured throatily, standing so close now he was actually touching her.

Causing fire to leap and flame through her veins like molten lava, her breathing ragged as she looked up at him.

Grey eyes shimmered like mercury, his gaze intense as it rested on her lips, his own breathing rapid and uneven.

'No, Nik—' Jinx only had time to protest achingly as his head lowered and his mouth took possession of hers.

Oh, yes, Nik, her body disagreed as it instinctively curved against the hardness of his. Jinx was the one to initiate the deepening of the kiss as she forgot everything else but the pleasure of being in this man's arms.

It had only been a few hours since they were last together like this, but even so they were hungry for each other, Nik's arms like steel bands about her waist, Jinx's hands moving restlessly up and down the long length of his spine as their lips and tongues explored and possessed, Jinx easily matching the desire that Nik made no effort to hide from her.

Nik was finally the one to pull back, his expression

regretful as he looked down at her, his hands still lightly linked at the base of her spine. 'Much as I'm enjoying this—and, believe me, I am enjoying it,' he drawled, 'at this particular moment I believe there may be several other things that need our immediate attention more.'

Jinx looked up at him with passion-drowsy eyes. 'Such as?'

He grimaced. 'The fact that there is a reporter and photographer outside—who, no matter what you might hope, aren't likely to be going anywhere soon. Which means—'

'Yes?' She had stiffened warily now, stepping back as she moved out of his arms to self-consciously straighten her hair, embarrassed at the way she kept falling into his arms.

Yes, she was attracted to him. Yes, she wanted him. But he was the last man she should keep responding to in this way.

Nik's look of regret deepened at her obvious withdrawal. 'Which means that you and your father will have to be the ones to leave. If only temporarily.'

Her eyes widened. 'That's ridiculous. It's you they're after, so when you leave, they will leave with you.'

She had moved house six months ago because continuing to stay at the family home had seemed to be badly affecting her father, his lapses more extreme as he shut himself off even from his surroundings; to move him again now—even temporarily!—was out of the question.

Nik raised dark brows. 'And if they don't?'

'They will,' she said flatly.

He shook his head. 'I wish I could be as sure of that as you appear to be...'

Jinx looked at him sharply. 'What do you mean?'

He shrugged. 'Just a hunch I have. Jinx, does it really

matter why they're hanging around out there?' he continued impatiently as she made to protest once again. 'The fact remains that they are there, and they have a lot more patience than you do. And your father isn't going to remain asleep upstairs for ever,' he added softly.

No, he would be down within the hour, and when he did come down he was unlikely to understand why it was she didn't answer the knocking on the front door. But where on earth was she supposed to go in order to avoid those people outside? Nik just didn't understand. There was no way she could take her father to the impersonality of a hotel, and it wasn't fair to just invite themselves to stay with friends, either.

She drew in a ragged breath. 'I still think that they will leave when you do,' she told him stubbornly.

He raised an eyebrow, signaling his disagreement with that statement. 'Shall we give it a try?'

Jinx looked at him with narrowed eyes, suspicious of his confident tone, as if he knew the reporter and photographer were waiting for her and not him.

But that couldn't be so. The only interest a reporter could possibly have in her was if they were to know of the J. I. Watson connection, and there was no way—

What about her meeting with Nik Prince this morning in the very public lounge of a large London hotel—a man already reported to be on the trail of the author J. I. Watson so that he could acquire the movie rights? What about her visit to James Stephens's office this morning?

She felt her heart sink as she faced the possibility that she could have been the one to lead the press to her home. It would be just too ironic if that were the case.

It was, also, primarily Nik Prince's fault, she decided angrily. If he hadn't been so persistent in the first place—

If he hadn't discovered the connection— If he hadn't followed her here—

'Don't bother,' she snapped, glaring her displeasure at him. 'Where do you suggest we go, then?' she demanded pointedly.

'Well, I've already given that some thought—'

'Why am I not surprised?' Jinx huffed.

Grey eyes gleamed warningly. 'There's no need to get angry with me—'

'Who else can I get angry with?'

Dark brows rose mockingly. 'And that's reason enough, is it—because I happen to be here?'

'For the moment—yes!' Her eyes flashed deeply violet. 'I'm still not convinced this wasn't all your fault. Everything was just fine before you came into my life—'

'Everything was *not* just fine!' he rapped out, eyes now a shimmering silver. 'Your father is very ill, and likely to remain so if he doesn't get professional help. Your own life is a mess—'

'I beg your pardon?' She stiffened resentfully.

'Look at you, Jinx. You have a job as a university tutor, but you can't do that at the moment because of taking care of your father. You're a famous author, but for the same reason you can't lay claim to that either.' He gave an impatient shake of his head. 'As for your personal life—'

'Stay out of my personal life, Nik!' she cut in coldly.

'I'm already in it—'

'Then I suggest you get *out* of it again!' she practically shouted. 'I don't need you, Nik, or your amateur psychiatry concerning my father; I believe I am the best judge of what is and isn't good for him! I just don't need you in my life…full stop!' She glared at him.

He drew in an angry breath. 'That wasn't the impression I got a few minutes ago—'

'Oh, let's bring that into it, shall we?' she scoffed. 'So I'm attracted to you; so what? Why is it that men feel they can differentiate between love and lust, but we women can't? Because I assure you that we can, Nik.' She gave a humourless laugh, angry with herself as much as him for the way she had once again given in to the desire she felt for him. '*I* can,' she claimed, her gaze challenging now as she met his.

Nik wanted to shake her. Wanted to grasp her shoulders and shake her until her teeth rattled.

Lust. She lusted after him?

No woman had ever said anything like that to him ever before—even if it had happened to be the truth! And, coming from Jinx, he found that he didn't like having it said to him now, either!

'What's the matter, Nik?' she taunted his silence. 'Don't you like having the tables turned on you?'

No, he damn well didn't! It was an unpleasant experience to be told that someone—Jinx!—lusted after him.

At the same time he could accept the irony of it. Wasn't it how he had always conducted his own personal relationships, feeling desire without the love?

Maybe it was, but that was still no explanation for the resentment he felt at having this five-foot-one-inch of a woman say the same thing to him...

He drew in a controlling breath. 'Not particularly,' he acknowledged. 'I'm also not sure it's the way for a nicely brought up young lady to be talking,' he mocked, knowing by the way the colour suddenly blazed in her cheeks that he had scored a direct hit with his barb.

But did he really want to score direct hits where Jinx

was concerned? Wasn't that just guaranteed to alienate her even more?

It was too late to realize that, Nik admitted ruefully as her expression became haughtily remote, violet eyes turning to icy blue. 'Probably not,' she accepted tersely. 'Now I really think it's time for you to leave, Nik.'

After which she would be at great pains to make sure the two of them *never* met again.

It was there in the resolve of her expression, in the coldness of her eyes, the defensive stance of her body.

But he knew where she lived now; he could always—

No, he couldn't, he accepted heavily. That would make him as bad as the reporter and photographer lying in wait for her outside.

Which brought him back to his initial point…

'Jinx, you really can't stay here—'

'I really can, Nik,' she insisted. 'In any case,' she continued firmly as he would have spoken, 'whether I decide to go or stay is really none of your business.'

He wanted to make it his business, wanted to pick Jinx up, throw her over his shoulder and carry her away from here. Be a regular caveman, in fact—which would go down with Jinx about as well as a lead balloon!

But the alternative was leaving her and her father here at the mercy of the press…

He drew in a deep breath. 'I have a friend—well, he's more like family, I suppose—it's a bit complicated,' he tried to explain, sure that now wasn't the right time to be discussing his sometimes complicated family tree. 'Have you ever heard of Ben Travis?' he asked instead.

'Should I have done?' Jinx returned cautiously.

'Probably not—although he is married to Marilyn Palmer.'

Jinx's eyes widened. 'The famous Hollywood actress?'

'The one and only.' Nik nodded. 'And Marilyn's daughter, Gaye, is married to the brother of Stazy's husband, Jordan Hunter.'

'The acting world is almost incestuous, isn't it?' Jinx scorned.

Nik felt the anger flare in his gaze, his mouth tightening to a thin line. 'Ben is a psychiatrist—'

'I've already told you, my father doesn't need a psychiatrist,' Jinx interrupted. 'Time and love are all he needs. And a little peace and quiet to go with it,' she added pointedly.

Meaning she really wanted him to leave now. Not that he hadn't thought she'd meant it in the first place, but now she absolutely wanted him out of her home. And her life...? Unfortunately, yes.

Nik sighed. 'Can I call you later?'

Jinx's gaze narrowed suspiciously. 'Why?'

He made an impatient movement. 'So that I can check that everything is okay!'

'And why shouldn't it be?'

'Jinx, will you just try being a little less defensive for a few minutes and actually think?' Nik exploded in frustration. 'If I leave—when I leave,' he amended as Jinx raised mocking brows, 'if, as I suspect, the reporter and her buddy continue to hang around outside, then I'm going to need to know about it—'

'Why?'

He really would strangle her in a minute! Which would achieve precisely nothing. But it might make him feel a lot better. If only fleetingly.

'Okay, let me put this another way,' he bit out, inwardly wondering how he could have been so aroused by her a few short minutes ago and now felt like throttling her! 'I am going to call you later to see how everything is.'

'You are?'

'Yes, I ar—am,' he corrected himself irritably.

She arched dark brows. 'And exactly how do you intend doing that when you don't have my telephone number?'

Go, Nik, he told himself. Now. Before you actually do reach out and do something you're going to regret!

'But I do have your telephone number, Jinx,' he couldn't resist assuring her triumphantly, at the same time congratulating himself on his perspicacity.

'I don't see how—'

'It's right there on your telephone,' he pointed out, at the same time giving a rueful wince as he waited for the explosion that was sure to come.

'You—you—' Jinx stared at him in disbelief. 'You really are one devious bast—'

'When are you going to realize I'm trying to *help* you?'

'When are you going to realize I don't *want* your help?' she returned furiously.

Nik stared down at her frustratedly, his hands clenched at his sides. 'Fine,' he bit out tersely, turning away abruptly, breathing deeply in an effort to calm down. Almost an impossibility when around this woman. 'I *will* call you later, though,' he added determinedly even as he left the study and strode forcefully down the hallway to the front door.

'Don't hold your breath on getting a reply,' Jinx called after him.

Nik came to a halt as he reached the door, forcing

himself not to retaliate, to just open the door and leave. But it wasn't easy.

In fact, as he was quickly learning, nothing was easy when it came to Jinx Nixon...

CHAPTER TEN

'HELLO…?' Jinx at once berated herself for sounding so hesitant as she answered the telephone call later that evening. After what he had said earlier, Nik Prince was sure to be the caller, and being hesitant around that man could only lead to him attempting to walk all over her—only attempting, of course, because he wouldn't succeed!

But he had been right about the reporter and photographer; the two of them were still waiting outside. In fact, the photographer had left for a brief time and returned with a car, in which the two of them now sat. It looked as if they were even eating hamburgers and drinking cola now, too. And waiting. And they appeared to be able to carry on doing just that for as long as it took for Jinx to have to finally leave the house, if only in order to buy food.

'Juliet?' a female voice answered. 'Juliet Nixon?'

Jinx's wariness increased at hearing this unfamiliar voice. 'Yes…'

'This is Stazy Hunter,' the woman responded. 'We met briefly at Susan and Leo's the other weekend.'

As if Jinx needed any reminding of who the other woman was! And where they had met wasn't the relevant point at the moment—the fact that this woman was Nik Prince's sister was!

She straightened defensively, unsure yet as to whether the other woman had got her telephone number from her brother or from Susan. 'What can I do for you, Mrs Hunter?'

'Please call me Stazy,' the other woman invited, her American accent softer and less pronounced than her brother's. 'And I believe your friends call you Jinx…?'

Yes, they did—but she very much doubted this woman was ever going to become her friend. 'I don't wish to sound rude, but exactly why have you telephoned me, Mrs—Stazy?' she corrected awkwardly; she would so much rather have kept things formal between the two of them, but at the same time Stazy Hunter sounded a genuinely warm and friendly person. So unlike her eldest brother!

The other woman gave a husky laugh. 'Don't worry, I don't have Nik breathing down my neck listening in on the conversation!'

That was something, at least! 'But he did ask you to telephone me?' Jinx said sharply.

'Yes, he—he's concerned about you…' Stazy Hunter told her ruefully.

'Then he has no right to be,' Jinx snapped. 'Something I have already told him once today!'

'So I believe,' Stazy chuckled appreciatively.

How much had Nik told his sister about the two of them? Not that there was a 'two of them', but she didn't particularly enjoy the thought of Nik discussing her with his sister at all.

'Is the reporter still there?' Stazy asked.

Jinx thought briefly of lying to the other woman, but what would be the point of doing that? Nik, when told of the conversation by his sister—as Jinx was sure he would be, even if he wasn't breathing down Stazy's neck right now!—would be sure to know that she was lying.

'Before you answer that,' Stazy Hunter continued warmly, 'may I just say how much I enjoyed your book. It made me cry as well as laugh,' she added sincerely.

Nik really had been confiding in his sister, hadn't he? Although it would probably have been a little difficult explaining his 'concern' for Jinx without telling the other woman of her connection to J. I. Watson.

Nevertheless, Jinx felt a warm glow at the other woman's praise for *No Ordinary Boy*. The books, five of them in all, had been written from the heart, and had made Jinx 'cry as well as laugh' too.

'Thank you,' she accepted huskily. 'And, yes, the reporter is still here, but it really isn't a problem.' At the moment…!

If the pair outside were set in for the duration, then it could definitely become a problem. And Jinx had a feeling that was exactly what they were going to do.

'Are you sure?' The frown could be heard in Stazy's voice. 'I know how intrusive the press can be.'

Well, she would, wouldn't she? Jinx acknowledged; Damien Prince, the legendary Hollywood actor, although dead for some time now, had been Stazy's father as well as Nik's, which meant the other woman had probably grown up surrounded by that intrusive press.

'They really aren't a problem,' Jinx repeated. 'It's very kind of you to have called in this way, Stazy,' she added briskly, 'but—'

'Kindness has little to do with it,' the other woman assured her. 'But I didn't just telephone to check up on the reporter. Nik thinks, and I have to agree with him, that it would be a good idea if you came here and stayed with me for a few days. You and your father, of course.'

Jinx frowned, totally speechless just at the idea of Nik putting forward the idea of inviting her to stay at the home of his sister.

'Then he has no right to think any such thing!' she finally answered incredulously. 'For one thing, I wouldn't dream of intruding on you and your family in that way—'

'Oh, you wouldn't be intruding,' Stazy Hunter assured her. 'In fact, Jordan is away on business for a few days, so I would quite enjoy having some female company.'

'For another, it's totally unnecessary,' Jinx added firmly. 'I don't mean to sound ungrateful, Stazy, it's just that—I'm well aware of whose idea this actually was! But please assure Nik that I don't need his help, that I'm perfectly capable of taking care of myself.' She hoped she didn't sound too rude to the other woman; she just wanted to make sure that Nik got the message she wanted him to receive—which was, 'Leave me alone!'

'Okay,' Stazy accepted, obviously not in the least offended. 'But I'll leave you my telephone number, anyway, shall I? Just in case.'

In case of what, Jinx had no idea, but she wrote the other woman's telephone number down anyway before saying goodbye.

She continued to sit by the telephone for several minutes after ending the call, a frown marring her creamy brow. Nik just couldn't stop interfering in her life, could he? Well, hopefully, that last message, relayed to him via his sister, might make him falter a little in his tracks. Although, knowing Nik, Jinx wouldn't count on it.

And did she really want him to just disappear completely from her life? She could be honest with herself, at least!

The answer was no, that even the last few hours of thinking about never seeing Nik again had left her with a heavy, oppressive feeling.

Could she really be falling in love with him?

Or was she already in love with him?

She heaved a big sigh, unable to deceive herself any

longer. She loved Nik, but the problem of *No Ordinary Boy* apart, there could never be a future for them together. Nik wasn't a man interested in for ever, and she was a woman who wouldn't settle for anything less.

Impasse.

Better to just leave things as they were. She would get over this in time. Wouldn't she…?

Not that there seemed much chance of her having that time when she looked out the window the next morning and found, not just the one reporter and photographer outside, but a dozen or more, cameras at the ready, at the moment all focused on the tall man getting out from behind the wheel of a dark green Jaguar.

Nik!

His expression was grim as he strode through the reporters and photographers, looking to neither left nor right, totally ignoring the barrage of questions being thrown at him, although it was impossible to stop the cameras flashing away.

In the circumstances, Jinx felt she had no option but to at least open the door to him, stepping out of the way as Nik turned to shut the door in the face of the more determined reporters who had followed him down the pathway. He looked cool and assured in a black shirt and faded denims, dark hair still looking wet from where he had taken a shower.

Which was more than could be said for Jinx. Having only just got out of bed, she was wearing a silky peach-coloured robe over a matching nightgown, her hair still tousled from sleep, her face completely make-upless.

'What on earth is going on?' she gasped. 'Where did they all come from?' She gave an airy wave in the direction of the front of the house.

Nik's expression remained grim. 'Have you seen the newspapers this morning?'

'Not yet. Mrs Holt usually brings it with her when she comes in the mornings, and it isn't time for her to arrive yet.' Which wasn't surprising, considering it was only eight o'clock in the morning!

He gave a shake of his head. 'If she has any sense, she won't bother!' he rasped. 'How long will it take you to collect up the things you and your father might need for at least a couple of days away?'

'Five minutes,' she answered dazedly. 'What was in the newspapers, Nik?' she asked as some of her normal composure started to come back to her.

'Actually, so far it's just the one—the one the initial reporter works for, presumably. But that won't remain the case after today. And you can definitely say goodbye to any idea of anonymity; there's a photograph to accompany the article speculating whether or not you're J. I. Watson!' He looked pointedly out of the window at the people milling around outside the house, obviously just waiting for a glimpse of the famous but elusive author.

Jinx put her hands up to her face as the enormity of what was happening washed over her. 'This is awful,' she groaned. 'Just awful!'

'Yes.' Nik didn't even attempt to soften the blow. 'You do realize you should have got out of here last night when Stazy asked you to?'

Her hands dropped back to her sides, her face pale now as she looked up at him. 'Don't you mean, when *you* asked me to?' she challenged.

'Me. Stazy. What the hell difference does it make who suggested it?' he growled. 'You should have damn well taken the opportunity to get out of here! As it is, the house is now surrounded like a three-ring circus!'

She could see that—she also had no idea how her father was going to react to all this when he came down in half an hour or so.

Her father.

No matter what she might personally want, she knew it was her father she had to think of now. And getting him away from here, from reporters and photographers, had to be her first priority.

'What do you want me to do?' she said briskly.

Nik raised surprised brows at her sudden acquiescence. 'Now you start being cooperative!'

Jinx felt the colour warm her cheeks. 'I had no idea it was going to—to escalate like this!' she defended impatiently.

'No, in your naivety, you probably didn't.'

Her eyes flashed deeply violet. 'We aren't all as world-weary and cynical as you, you know!'

Nik became suddenly still, looking down at her with hooded eyes. 'Is that how you see me?' he asked slowly. 'As world-weary and cynical?'

'Well, aren't you?' Jinx flushed uncomfortably, knowing she was behaving ungratefully after the way Nik had taken the trouble to come here—in spite of her clearly telling him to go away and stay away!—and try to help her out of this mess.

Despite what she was saying to Nik, she was grateful for his help. She knew that she would never have known how to handle this situation on her own.

She just couldn't tell Nik how grateful she was—not when she was also in love with him!

Nik, giving her accusation some thought, totally missed that briefly bewildered expression on Jinx's face.

World-weary?

And cynical?

Yes, he was both those things. But when he looked at Jinx, so incredibly young-looking without make-up and her hair all tousled from sleep, none of that seemed to matter any more.

'Jinx…!'

She gave a startled look at the groan of longing that escaped him, the colour slowly draining from her face as she continued to stare at him.

This wasn't the time for this, Nik knew. He should be concentrating on getting Jinx and her father away from here. But at the moment, having spent a totally sleepless night because of the way the two of them had parted yesterday and the fact that Jinx had refused Stazy's offer of help, Nik felt that if he didn't take Jinx in his arms, feel the softness of her lips against his, the warmth of her body curved against him, he might go quietly insane!

She felt as good against him as he remembered—better! Her lips were soft and delicious beneath his. The fluttering caress of her hands against his nape before she clung to him spread a sensual warmth through the whole of his body. As for how Jinx felt beneath the silky material of her robe…!

God, he wanted this woman!

He might try to deny it, keep telling himself that his interest in her was purely business, but his body knew better. As for his heart—

Nik pulled back sharply, total denial in his face as he stared down into her drowsily aroused face. He didn't have a heart—goodness knew enough women had told him that in the past! What he felt for Jinx was desire, pure and simple. It didn't need to be complicated by things like love!

'I think you had better go and get dressed,' he said

gruffly, moving away and thrusting his hands into his denims pockets so that he shouldn't be tempted to reach for her again.

His own feelings apart, hadn't Jinx made it perfectly obvious how she felt about him? Of course she had. She only 'lusted' after him. God, how he still wanted to shake her for saying that!

Jinx flinched as if he had physically struck her, her face paler than ever as she hastily tightened the belt on her robe. 'Yes,' she acknowledged woodenly. 'I— How am I supposed to get out of here, without running into— into those people outside?' She gave a hunted look in the direction of the front of the house.

'Leave it to me,' he assured her. 'While you're upstairs dressing,' he added impatiently as Jinx stared at him levelly, obviously having no intention of going up the stairs until he had explained exactly what he intended doing, 'I intend going outside and telling them that a statement will be forthcoming in the next fifteen minutes or so—'

'No way!' She shuddered with feeling, at the same time seeming to sink back into her robe. 'I have no intention of going out there and—'

'Of course you don't,' Nik grated. 'If you listened to what I said, you will realize I didn't actually say *who* would be making that statement.'

She blinked, staring up at him uncertainly now.

'Right.' He nodded. 'Hopefully all the reporters will then gather at the front of the house in anticipation of the statement. And while I'm outside making that statement, you and your father will be leaving by the back door.'

Jinx still looked bewildered. 'Leaving how?'

He wanted to take her in his arms again, wanted to smooth away that worried frown, to reassure her that everything was going to be all right. But his own confused emotions kept him from doing that. And the fact that those violet-blue eyes, as if she were aware of exactly what he wanted to do, were now glittering warningly!

'My brother will have arrived out the back in a second car by then—'

'Zak?' She looked and sounded horrified.

'Not this time,' Nik drawled, scowling slightly as he wondered if Jinx's horror was because of who Zak was or because she was yet another woman besotted with his glamorous younger brother.

He was being paranoid, he told himself pityingly. That, and jealous at the thought of Jinx finding any other man attractive.

'This will be my youngest brother, Rik,' Nik told her.

'The screenwriter?'

'The one and only.'

'My, my,' Jinx taunted. 'And to what do we owe the honour of all these Princes?'

Nik's mouth tightened. 'I already told you that we all came over initially for our nephew's christening. But Zak stayed on to discuss his next movie. Rik is visiting with Stazy for a few weeks. And I—'

'I think we all know why *you're* still here!' she snapped.

He gave a dismissive shrug; having an argument with Jinx now wasn't going to help anyone. 'Rik has never been as keen as Zak to have his photograph splashed all over the newspapers.'

Her mouth twisted ruefully. 'Then that makes two of us!'

'Yes,' he confirmed tersely.

'Doesn't Rik mind? After all, he doesn't know me from Adam.'

'I know you,' Nik stated without apology for his arrogance. They were a close family, always had been, and what affected one affected all of them. So when he had asked Rik for his help today his brother hadn't questioned the 'whys', had just got in the second car and followed him here. 'Time is ticking on, Jinx,' he reminded her.

'Yes.' She nodded, once again looking up at him uncertainly. 'This really is very kind of you, Nik.' Her voice was husky.

Sensually so, Nik realized with that now-familiar ache. Damn it, did everything about this woman have to arouse him?

'Not really,' he dismissed curtly. 'The photograph in the newspaper is of you leaving the publishing house yesterday, so I guess I owe you one.'

'Oh. Right.' She smiled shakily. 'Fine. I—I'll go and get dressed, then.'

'I should,' he mocked. 'Unless you want to cause even more of a sensation!'

Nik watched her as she hurried up the stairs, admiring the brief glimpse of a shapely leg as she reached the top before disappearing into a bedroom.

He turned away, his hands tightly clenched at his sides as he drew in a controlling breath, knowing he couldn't go with his instinct to follow Jinx upstairs to her bedroom, take her into his arms and make love to her until they were either sated with each other or simply died from lack of food.

In any case, he had a feeling Jinx Nixon was going to be the death of him—one way or another!

CHAPTER ELEVEN

JINX gave the man seated beside her a sideways glance as he drove behind the wheel of the silver Mercedes that had been waiting for them at the back of the house. Just as Nik had promised it would be.

But, then, she wouldn't have expected anything else, would she?

This man, the youngest of the Prince brothers, was much more like Nik to look at than Zak, being dark-haired, too, although his eyes were blue. But other than getting out of the car to put the single bag that Jinx had brought with her into the boot, and to see her father safely seated in the back of the car—her father actually seemed to be enjoying this change in his routine, quite happy as he sat back looking out of the car window!—Rik Prince hadn't said a word.

Jinx cleared her throat before speaking lightly. 'You must wonder what on earth is going on!'

He shrugged broad shoulders, his attention remaining on the road ahead. 'I'm sure if Nik wants me to know then he'll tell me in his own good time.'

She raised auburn brows. 'Is that the way it usually works?'

Rik gave her a sideways look. 'The way what usually works, Miss Nixon?'

Jinx gave him an uneasy glance, realizing that there was a lot more to Rik Prince than initially met the eye. He was more like Nik than she had realized, and not just in looks. He had managed to convey quite a lot in that

133

question than had actually been said. He didn't smile as easily as Nik, either—and Nik wasn't exactly known for his jollity!

'This.' She gave a pointed shrug, that one word encompassing the press gathered outside her home, her escape out of the back door while Nik kept the press otherwise occupied at the front of the house, this drive through London to goodness knew where—she had completely forgotten to ask Nik where his brother was taking her!

'This is a first for me, Miss Nixon,' Rik Prince told her evenly. 'For Nik too, I suspect,' he added with a touch of wry humour in his voice.

Jinx's eyes widened. 'But you're all so famous; you must have problems like this with the press all the time.'

His mouth relaxed into a rueful smile. 'I wasn't referring to the need to avoid the press.'

'Then what—? Never mind,' she dismissed quickly, having decided she probably didn't want to hear the answer to that particular question; it was bound to involve Nik in some way, and she was desperately trying to keep things in perspective as far as he was concerned.

For one thing, she had to try and remember that Nik had an ulterior motive for helping her in this way, and that that motive wasn't exactly unselfish. For another, she had to keep remembering that, although she had realized she was in love with him, Nik certainly wasn't in love with her.

Which wasn't all that easy to do when he kept coming to her rescue in this way!

'Can I ask where you're taking us?' Jinx opted for a neutral question rather than pursuing the previous subject.

'Initially to my sister Stazy's. But after that I'm sure

Nik will take you wherever you want to go,' he said before Jinx could protest this plan.

Which she had been about to do! At the moment she felt as if she had slightly lost control of what was happening in her life, as if she and her father were being drawn in by the Prince family, to be cocooned in their protective circle.

The only problem with that was they were just as likely to be spat out again afterwards, when they were of no more use.

'Fine,' Jinx accepted tautly, turning to look out of the car window herself now.

She could always go to a hotel with her father, she supposed, although, as she had already told Nik the previous day, it was far from an ideal solution with her father the way that he was. Maybe Susan and Leo would—

'I really wouldn't worry about it, Miss Nixon,' Rik assured her softly. 'At least talk to Nik first before making any immediate decisions.'

She turned back to him, her smile derisive. 'We both know that if Nik has already decided I will stay at your sister Stazy's house, then that is precisely where I will be expected to stay!'

He raised dark brows. 'Is that really such a problem?'

'When it comes to conceding to Nik's arrogance— yes!' she said with feeling.

Rik gave a humourless smile. 'Aren't you being a little ungrateful, in the circumstances?'

Jinx felt the warm colour in her cheeks at this man's gentle rebuke. Yes, she knew she must sound ungrateful, it was just that— Just that nothing, she acknowledged heavily. Nik hadn't had to come and help her out this morning; he could just as easily have left her to her own devices. In which case she would still be a prisoner in her own home!

'I'm sorry,' she sighed. 'It's just—Nik can be a little overbearing at times.'

'Tell me about it!' Rik's smile warmed. 'But, in his defence, I would like to add that he usually means well. He just doesn't always ask before following a particular course of action.'

Jinx returned his smile, starting to like this youngest of the three Prince brothers. Quieter, more serious, he had a reserved sense of humour, a quiet reassurance, that appealed to her.

'I'm the screenwriter of the family, by the way,' he told her gently, one dark brow raised questioningly.

Jinx sobered, her expression noncommittal. 'I know.'

'I would love to work on *No Ordinary Boy*,' Rik murmured.

She stiffened, well aware of her father seated in the back of the car, even if he did still give every appearance of sitting back and enjoying the drive. 'Look, Rik, I—'

'You don't want to talk about it.' He nodded understandingly. 'No, I can see how that might be a problem for you.'

Jinx blinked at his easy calm. 'You can…?'

'Oh, yes.' He gave her a sympathetic smile. 'My big brother still has it wrong, doesn't he?'

Jinx felt herself go cold as the colour drained from her face. 'What do you mean?' Although she was very much afraid she knew exactly what he meant!

'Nik explained before we left this morning about your family—tragedy.' He glanced pointedly in the driving-mirror at her father seated in the back seat.

Jinx was so tense she ached. 'And?'

'I'm a writer too, Jinx,' he told her softly.

'And?' she prompted again.

'We can talk later,' Rik murmured huskily. 'This obviously isn't the time to talk about this.'

No, of course it wasn't, not with her father within earshot. But the two of them did need to talk. Rik Prince was implying that he had guessed the real truth behind the writing of *No Ordinary Boy*—something that no other person had.

She swallowed hard. 'Rik—'

'It can wait, Jinx.' He reached out and briefly covered her hand with his. 'We're at Stazy's now,' he added briskly as he waited for the electronic gates to open before driving up the long gravel driveway to the imposing Victorian house owned by the Hunters. 'Stazy needs the room for the half a dozen kids she plans on having,' he explained affectionately as the three of them got out of the car.

'I hope her husband feels the same way!' Jinx joined in the easy conversation, while all the time she was deeply aware of Rik's earlier comments.

She didn't know how, or why, but it was pretty obvious that Rik Prince had guessed the truth about *No Ordinary Boy*, that he somehow knew she was no more the author J. I. Watson than her father had been!

Not that Jinx had too much time to think about that as Stazy Hunter came out of the house and down the steps to greet them, almost immediately followed by the crunch of gravel on the driveway as the green Jaguar, with a grim-faced Nik behind the wheel, arrived only seconds behind them.

'I went a circuitous route, just in case,' Rik explained as Jinx looked surprised to see Nik there so soon. 'And stop looking so worried,' he whispered so that the others didn't overhear. 'For the moment it's just our secret, okay?'

No, it wasn't okay! How long was that 'moment' going to last? Did Rik intend speaking to her again first before confiding in his older brother?

'All right, Jinx?'

She blinked up at Nik as he stood beside her, a concerned frown between enigmatic grey eyes. 'Fine. I— Was everything okay? At the house, I mean?' she said awkwardly, aware of his watching—and listening— brother and sister.

Nik gave a humourless smile. 'Well, I've probably totally annoyed the majority of the tabloid press by helping you to escape out the back door—but other than that…? Yes, everything's fine.'

Jinx hadn't really given any thought to the fact that by helping her in this way Nik was leaving himself open to a deluge of publicity…

But she thought of it now. 'I don't believe I've thanked you properly yet for coming to my aid this morning,' she said huskily.

He raised a mocking eyebrow. 'I believe you did mention "how kind it was of me"!'

Jinx looked up at him blankly for several seconds, and then she began to smile as she realized he was teasing her for how pompous she must have sounded earlier. Considering the man had just thoroughly kissed her seconds earlier, doubly pompous!

'Er—if I could just interrupt for a few seconds…?' Stazy inserted. 'I believe your father might like to go inside and have a cup of tea and possibly some breakfast?'

Jinx dragged her gaze away from Nik's with effort, turning to look at her father as he stood beside Rik admiring the fish in the pond in the front garden. Colour warmed her cheeks as she acknowledged what Stazy had obviously realized; for the duration of those few minutes' conversation with Nik, she had completely forgotten everyone else but him! Including her father…

'Of course. Sorry.' She grimaced. 'You must think me very rude.' She smiled hesitantly at Stazy.

'Not at all,' the other woman dismissed. 'Nik has this effect on people, I believe.'

'Ha ha, very funny,' he drawled, at the same time taking a light hold of Jinx's arm. 'As it happens, Stazy, I don't think any of us have had time for breakfast this morning.'

She really had inconvenienced everyone, hadn't she? Jinx realized with a frown. The least she could do now was be a little more gracious considering the help Nik and his family had given her this morning.

Although that wouldn't change the fact that she had to talk to Rik Prince, in private, at the earliest opportunity!

Nik could see the different emotions flittering across Jinx's beautiful expressive face; knew, despite her thank-you of a few minutes ago, that she was still having difficulty coming to terms with the fact that it had been him who had come to her rescue this morning.

His mouth tightened ominously as he remembered almost choking over his morning coffee as he'd seen the photograph and headlines on the first of the pile of newspapers he had delivered to him in his hotel room every morning.

COULD THIS BE J. I. WATSON? the headline had shouted, and beneath had been a photograph of Jinx as she'd left Stephens Publishing yesterday.

And it was unmistakably Jinx, her red hair gleaming

like copper, her expression intense as she hurried to get in the waiting taxi. Hurried to get away from him...

Not that the last part had seemed in the least important earlier this morning; Jinx needed his help, and, whether she wanted it or not, she was going to get it!

Although now that she was away from the chaos that existed at her home she definitely looked less than pleased at finding herself here.

'Breakfast,' Nik told her decisively, maintaining his hold on her arm as he urged her to follow the others into the house. 'Nothing ever looks as bad on a full stomach, my mother used to say,' he added teasingly as Jinx looked up at him.

'Mine too,' she acknowledged heavily. 'But mothers can't always be right, can they?'

'Mine usually was,' Nik insisted, seeing Jinx seated at the breakfast table before reaching over to pour her a cup of coffee. 'Maybe coffee will do the trick,' he said, receiving a sceptical grimace for his trouble. 'What would your father like?' he asked, the older man still looking completely unruffled by his new surroundings as he smiled benignly.

'I'll see to him,' Jinx answered abruptly, getting up to move to her father's side.

Nik's gaze narrowed on the older man as he turned to respond to Jinx's gentle enquiry. Jackson Nixon had been an intelligent man and Nik simply couldn't accept that there wasn't a way to help him get back to that.

'Perhaps you shouldn't interfere, Nik.' Rik spoke softly at his side.

Nik turned and scowled at his brother. 'Don't you think that someone has to?' he grated.

Rik seemed to give the idea some thought. 'Not necessarily, no,' he finally answered slowly.

'Not necessarily!'

'Calm down, Nik,' Rik soothed. 'I merely meant that it isn't really any of your business. Or is it…?' he queried softly.

Nik's mouth tightened, his gaze impaling his youngest brother. Rik had always tended to keep things to himself, didn't talk too often, but when he did people took notice of him. As Nik was doing now.

Perhaps Rik was right, and Jackson Nixon's mental health wasn't any of his business, but—

But what?

With her father like this, and Jinx being the only close family that he had left, there was no way that she would ever allow herself to have a life of her own. And that included becoming involved with anyone. With him…

Nik suddenly decided that he didn't like the too-innocent expression he could see on Rik's face. 'Have you talked to Zak recently?'

His brother raised dark brows. 'Should I have done?'

Nik gave a humourless smile. 'When are you two going to grow up?'

Rik gave an unconcerned shrug. 'When we finally see our big brother topple as he falls in love?'

Nik gave a derisive snort. 'You'll have a long wait!'

'Do you think so?' Rik mused before turning to give Jinx a smile as she sat back down at the table, not next to Nik this time, but on Rik's other side.

Nik stiffened. Now why had she done that? It was further away from her father—but further away from him too, Nik acknowledged frustratedly. Damn it, he had never met a woman who was so stubborn.

Never met a woman like Jinx ever before…

And that was his problem, he decided as he watched Jinx through narrowed eyes. She was unique. Totally unlike anyone else he had ever met. Forced a response from him that he had never known before, either!

Even now, just sitting in the same room as her, he was totally aware of her, of the slender elegance of her hands as she buttered a croissant, of the soft pout of her lips as she put the croissant down untouched to sip from her coffee-cup—damn it, was it normal to feel jealous of a knife and a piece of china?

Because Nik did. He wanted the gentle caress of her hands on him, wanted the feel of her lips crushed beneath his, the slenderness of her body curved perfectly into his.

No, this wasn't normal, Nik decided as Jinx turned to give Rik a look beneath long lashes and a wave of black rage instantly washed over him. It wasn't normal to be jealous of Jinx just looking at another man. Not just any man, but his own brother, for goodness' sake!

'You aren't eating, Nik,' Stazy prompted from his other side.

He drew in a deeply controlling breath before turning to face his sister. 'Sorry, no appetite,' he apologized.

Stazy glanced past him. 'Is Jinx going to stay here, do you think?'

He shrugged. 'You would have to ask her that,' he rasped. 'I'm the last person Jinx would confide her plans to!' He knew that he sounded bad-tempered and impatient—and not a little petulant? he questioned ruefully—but that seemed to be becoming the norm where Jinx was concerned.

Stazy shot him an amused glance. 'Finally met your match when it comes to stubbornness, have you?'

'I don't even come close to Jinx's bloody-mindedness!' He scowled darkly.

If anything, Stazy looked even more amused. 'Oh, I wouldn't be too sure about that,' she said.

'Thanks!'

'You're welcome,' Stazy returned cheerily.

Nik turned to give Jinx another glance, only to find her once again looking at Rik. A Rik who turned at that moment and gave her a gently reassuring smile as he softly encouraged her to eat her croissant, Jinx responding to that encouragement.

Hell, what had happened between these two during that half-an-hour car journey?

Because something certainly had; he had never seen Rik this tenderly solicitous, or Jinx this compliant!

He was completely jealous of his own brother, Nik realized disgustedly.

Now that really was a first. And to be jealous of Rik, too. As a family, they had come to expect Zak to flit from one woman to another, but, as far as any of them were aware, Rik hadn't been seriously interested—and that was the only sort of interest Rik ever showed!—in a woman for years.

Although, if the admiration in his gaze as he looked at Jinx, and the warmth of his manner as he poured her another cup of coffee, were anything to go by, Rik was certainly interested now!

No!

Every particle of Nik rose up in protest at the thought of Rik ever being involved with Jinx. She was *his*, damn it—

Exactly what did that mean?

His? In what way was she his? In no way, came the unequivocal answer!

And yet the thought of Jinx with any other man, his brother Rik included, was enough to fill him with murderous rage. Well…maybe not murderous—but he would certainly want to do someone physical damage if he ever saw Jinx with another man!

'Are you sure it isn't going to inconvenience you?' Jinx was obviously answering something Stazy had said to her now.

'Not in the least,' Stazy replied. 'As I told you on the telephone last night, Jordan is away for a few days, and I would appreciate the company.'

'What does that make me?' Rik put in mockingly.

'I meant female company, silly,' Stazy chided, the two of them grinning at each other affectionately.

Meaning that both of them missed Jinx's reaction to the fact that Rik was staying here at Stazy's too.

But Nik was all too aware of the look of relief that flitted across Jinx's expressive face.

Filling him with a depth of anger he had never known before.

CHAPTER TWELVE

JINX could feel the relief wash over her as Stazy finally left her to the privacy of the bedroom she was to occupy for the duration of her stay here. A short duration, if she had anything to say about it.

The last half an hour, as Stazy had lingered over her cup of coffee before baby Sam woke up and demanded her attention, had seemed like pure purgatory as far as Jinx was concerned, all too aware of Nik's brooding silence as he sat further down the table.

What on earth was wrong with him?

It had been his idea to bring her here, but his silence seemed to imply that he now regretted that impulse.

Because it brought her closer into his family? Because he had realized it might somehow give her the idea that the attraction he felt towards her was more than that?

He need have no worries on that score! She knew exactly what his interest in her was—she wasn't so simple-minded as to imagine that the attraction between them would ever lead to a wedding dress and orange blossom!

But he had been singularly uncommunicative—even for Nik!—since their arrival here. Didn't—?

Jinx turned sharply as the bedroom door suddenly opened, every inch of her tensing as Nik stood silhouetted in the doorway. 'I always thought it was polite to knock...' She frowned across at him.

'Sorry,' he bit out unrepentantly, at the same time stepping further into the room and closing the door softly behind him.

A deceptive softness, as the grim expression on his face was anything but calm. Or reassuring.

Jinx straightened, eyeing him warily. 'What do you want, Nik?'

'What do I want?' he repeated mockingly. 'What I really want is never to have met you! What I really want is to forget that I ever did meet you! What I really want—'

'I think I get the picture, Nik,' she cut in sharply, inwardly flinching with every word he uttered.

She was in love with this man—and he wished that he had never met her!

'I doubt it,' he growled, thrusting his hands into his trouser pockets. 'Jinx, exactly what is going on between you and my little brother?'

She frowned. 'Zak?'

'You know exactly which brother I'm referring to, Jinx, so stop playing games!' Nik scowled. 'You and Rik exchanged coy looks all through breakfast—'

'Now you're being ridiculous!' Jinx interrupted. Coy looks? She hadn't been aware of Nik's gaze on the two of them, but she did know that on her part they were more likely to be wary looks than coy ones; Rik Prince had implied he knew altogether too much!

'Am I?' Nik challenged, his face all hard angles. 'Hell, the two of you were only alone together for half an hour or so in the car, and yet my little brother can't seem to take his eyes off you!'

'That's rubbish, and you know it—' She broke off as Nik moved to stand far too close to her than was comfortable, her breath catching in her throat as she looked up at him. 'I barely know Rik,' she protested.

Nik's mouth twisted derisively. 'You barely know me either—but I have trouble keeping my hands off you!'

As if to prove his point he reached out to put his arms around her and pull her into the hardness of his body. 'Don't mess with my younger brother, Jinx,' he warned her, grey eyes glittering silver.

She couldn't breathe at all now, totally aware of the hard length of Nik's body as she curved softly against him.

His gaze narrowed. 'Did you hear me?'

'I heard you!' she assured him, her voice rising slightly in her confusion at being held so close to this man. She shook her head. 'Rik isn't interested in me, Nik. And I'm not interested in him, either,' she added quickly as she saw the way his eyes darkened dangerously. 'If you must know, I— He reminds me a little of you!'

Nik became suddenly still, his eyes like silver shards of glass as he seemed to look into her soul. 'What's that supposed to mean?'

Jinx shrugged. 'You're the one with all the answers— you work it out!'

Although a part of her hoped that he never would. It was one thing to know that she was in love with him, quite another for Nik to realize it too!

Nik continued to look at her searchingly for several long seconds. 'You have a very kissable mouth, do you know that?' he finally murmured huskily.

She swallowed hard. 'So do you,' she answered softly, her gaze transfixed on the sensuality of his full lower lip.

His eyes widened. 'I do?'

She fought the impulse to reach up on tiptoe and explore that sensuality with her lips and tongue. 'You do.'

He drew in a sharp breath. 'Jinx, when all this is over—'

'Will it ever be?' she dismissed heavily, looking away,

the moment of intimacy passing as quickly as it had arrived.

'I hope so.' He nodded grimly before giving an impatient sigh. 'I have to go out and see to a couple of things,' he rasped, releasing her to move abruptly away. 'Will you be okay here while I'm gone?'

Jinx gave a scornful laugh, towards herself as much as him as she felt the loss of his warmth. 'Well, I'm not going to wither and fade away because you aren't here, if that's what you mean?'

He snorted. 'No, that's not what I meant! What I'm really asking is if you can delay making any other plans until I come back later?'

He was asking? Not telling, but asking? That had to be a first!

She gave an inclination of her head. 'I'm sure I can do that,' she answered slowly.

'Good.' He nodded his satisfaction before striding over to the bedroom door. He paused after opening it. 'Try to stay out of trouble for a couple of hours, hmm?'

'Try to—!' Jinx spluttered indignantly. The most 'trouble' she intended getting into was asking Rik for an explanation of his earlier remarks.

'It does seem to follow you around,' Nik drawled.

She glared at him. 'Only since I met you!'

'Well, it's nice to know I've had some sort of impact on your life!' He chuckled throatily, closing the door carefully behind him as he left.

Well, really! First he accused her of flirting with his younger brother, and then he had the cheek to tell her to stay out of trouble!

Until she'd met Nik Prince she had never been in trouble, her life quietly uneventful.

Boringly so?

She had never thought so. Although it was certainly going to become so once Nik had gone from her life.

She sat down heavily on the bed just at the thought of it. He was just so overpoweringly there, larger than life, that it was impossible to be anything other than completely aware of him.

Much as she fought against his arrogance and his domineering attitude, she had no idea how was she going to feel when he was no longer around.

Although she could take a guess…

Arriving back at Stazy's three hours later, and finding Jinx and Rik ensconced in the kitchen preparing lunch together, was not conducive to calming Nik's already volatile mood!

'Well, isn't this cosy?' he rapped out with barely suppressed fury.

'Oh, hi, Nik.' Rik turned to greet him, smiling blandly. 'Stazy's upstairs bathing Sam.'

He didn't give a damn where Stazy was—the fact that Rik and Jinx were here together, after he had warned Jinx earlier this morning to stay away from his brother, was enough to make his blood boil.

Especially as he had just spent a frustrating morning trying to get to the bottom of this latest development in Jinx's already complicated life!

'Hello, Nik,' she said huskily, at the same time eyeing him warily.

As well she might! He had been chasing all over London on her behalf for the last three hours, trying to track down the original reporter, and her source. The fact that Jinx didn't know that was what he had been doing was totally irrelevant!

'Hello,' he grated, his gaze meeting hers challengingly.

She blinked. 'I— We're having chicken curry for lunch.' She made an ineffectual gesture towards the apple she was dicing to add to the mixture frying on the hob.

His mouth twisted. 'I can smell that.'

'Had a good morning, Nik?' Rik broke into the tension that was thickening by the second.

Nik turned glacial eyes on his brother, wondering if Rik could possibly have guessed what he had been doing this morning. 'As it happens—no,' he rasped. 'I need to talk to you later, Jinx,' he added firmly.

'I—er—fine.' She nodded, frowning her puzzlement.

'Where is your father?' Nik looked around pointedly at the otherwise empty kitchen.

'In the garden.' Jinx's frown deepened at his obvious hostility. 'He likes watching the fish in the pond—didn't you see him when you came in?' she realized sharply, her body tensing in alarm.

The garden and driveway had been completely empty when he'd come in seconds ago; he would certainly have seen Jackson Nixon if he had been there.

'Oh, no!' Jinx cried as she easily read the denial in his face, dropping the knife she was holding to run out into the hallway.

Nik put his hand on Rik's arm as he would have hurried after her. 'I want to talk to you later, too,' he told his brother grimly.

Rik looked completely unperturbed. 'That sounds like fun! Now shouldn't we help Jinx look for her father?' he suggested as Nik opened his mouth to assure him of just how little fun it was going to be.

His jaw clamped together in annoyance. 'Yes,' he grated, the two of them following Jinx out the front door.

Jinx was obviously frantic, her face pale, unshed tears almost blinding her as she looked up at Nik. 'He isn't here!' she choked. 'I've looked everywhere, and—' She broke off as two men came round the side of the house, one her father, the other man known to Nik but not to Jinx. 'Oh, thank God,' she breathed her relief as she turned into Nik's arms, her face resting against the hardness of his chest as she held onto him. 'Thank God!'

Well, at least it was him she had turned to in her distress. Although the look of mocking derision on Rik's face as he glanced at his brother over the top of Jinx's fiery head seemed to taunt Nik for thinking she would have done anything else.

But what was he to think? Rik was the most reserved of the three brothers, preferring to keep himself and his life totally private. He didn't make friends easily, and yet he and Jinx were comfortable enough in each other's company for it to seem as if they had known each other for years.

Exactly, the deepening mockery on Rik's face seemed to say.

Because the last thing Nik felt was comfortable in Jinx's company; often angry, always frustrated, his senses heightened and attuned to her every movement, but never, ever comfortable!

'There you are!' Jinx released herself to hurry over to her father, smiling brightly in an effort to try to hide her anxiety of a few seconds ago.

'Jackson and I were just taking a stroll round the garden,' the other man told her soothingly.

'That's nice,' she returned absently, her whole attention centred on her father at the moment.

Although Nik had a feeling that wasn't going to last for too long, and once she learned the other man's identity...!

Nik winced as he imagined the fireworks that were

going to follow once she did know. He also knew it would be no good claiming his innocence; Jinx seemed to take delight in thinking the worst of him, and his motives.

'Are you here for lunch, Ben?' Rik asked.

'Not today, no,' the older man answered smilingly. 'I just thought I would look in on Stazy and Sam on my way to meet Marilyn for lunch.'

Rik nodded. 'Stazy was upstairs bathing Sam, but I expect she's finished by now.' He fell into step beside the older man as they began to walk towards the house, shooting Nik a knowing look before nodding pointedly towards Jinx and her father, obviously intending for Nik to accompany the pair into the house.

In truth, Nik was reluctant to look at Jinx, could feel her accusing glare from ten feet away, knew from that glare that she had already added two and two together where Ben was concerned and come up with the correct answer of four. Except it wasn't quite correct. Yes, Ben was the Ben Travis he had already mentioned to Jinx as a possibility for trying to help her father. But no, the older man certainly wasn't here at Nik's invitation; he knew Jinx well enough to know she wouldn't thank him for his interference. Not in that situation, anyway…

Although the furious expression on her face when he finally did chance a glance in her direction assured him that she wasn't going to give him the opportunity to even try to explain…

CHAPTER THIRTEEN

'How dare you? How dare you?' Jinx was so angry, she was shaking with the emotion.

It didn't matter that Ben Travis had spent the whole of his half an hour visit playing with baby Sam and talking mainly to members of the Prince family; Jinx was still very aware of who he was, what he was, and the fact that the man studied her father whenever he thought no one else was watching him.

Jinx had picked at her lunch, eating little, talking even less, just waiting for the opportunity when she could speak to Nik alone. Like now!

'I told you I didn't want any help for my father,' she continued forcefully, the two of them alone in the sitting-room, her father taking his afternoon nap, Rik having opted to accompany Stazy while she went shopping. 'I told you that quite categorically,' she snapped. 'And yet you still went against my decision and invited a psychiatrist here—'

'I didn't invite him, Jinx,' Nik denied, completely relaxed as he sat in one of the comfortable armchairs watching Jinx as she impatiently paced the room.

'I don't believe you!' She glared. 'It's too much of a coincidence that we should have to come here this morning, and that a couple of hours later Ben Travis just *happened* to call round—'

'For reasons I'm not about to go into, Ben calls around all the time,' Nik cut in, grey eyes starting to glitter silver. 'And I don't appreciate being called a liar, Jinx,' he added coolly. 'If I had invited Ben here to take a look at your father to see if there's anything he can do, then I would tell you so. But as I didn't...' He gave a dismissive shrug.

Jinx's resolve wavered slightly at his complete implacability, but then she remembered the way he had disappeared this morning, on the pretext of 'having things to do', and the fact that Ben Travis had arrived here so conveniently, and she knew, no matter what Nik might claim to the contrary, that it couldn't just be a coincidence, not when Nik had already mentioned the possibility of consulting the other man concerning her father's condition.

'He spoke to me before he left, you know,' Jinx bit out. 'Took me quietly to one side and told me that if I would like him to try talking with my father at any time, Stazy has his telephone number.' An offer that she had politely, but firmly, refused!

Nik gave an impatient sigh. 'I can guess what your answer was to that suggestion. But whether or not I'm responsible for Ben's visit here today—which, incidentally, I'm not,' he insisted, 'what is so wrong with the idea of Ben talking with your father?'

'I— It— You—'

What *was* so wrong with it? Just the fact that it was Nik who had suggested it? Or did she genuinely believe that it would be a waste of Ben Travis's time as well as her father's?

'As it happens, Ben spoke to me before he left too.' Nik spoke quietly as she desperately sought the answers to her own questions.

'What a surprise!' Jinx taunted.

Nik drew in a sharply angry breath, his mouth thinning with the same emotion. 'Believe what you like, Jinx, but

I would have thought that you would want to do something about your father's mental health—'

'Of course I want to do something about it!' she cut in furiously.

'Just not at what you believe is my instigation?' Nik guessed scornfully.

Machination more aptly described this man's behaviour when it came to getting something that he wanted. As she already knew only too well!

'You're irrelevant,' she dismissed with deliberate rudeness, knowing she had scored a direct hit as a nerve began to pulse in Nik's rigidly clenched jaw. 'The fact of the matter is that I don't want to make my father's condition any worse than it already is—'

'And his talking to Ben is going to do that?'

'I don't know, do I?' she wailed.

These last eighteen months of being completely responsible for her father's health and well-being had taken their toll on her own nerves, but the last thing she wanted was to make her father's life any more difficult than it already was.

Nik sat forward in his chair, his gaze compelling. 'Then shouldn't you at least give it a try? Jinx, you can't believe he can actually stay the way that he is?' He gave a disbelieving shake of his head. 'In fact, Ben has already warned me that he probably won't,' he continued determinedly. 'It was the trauma of your mother's and brother's deaths that put him in this state. Another shock could just as easily bring him out of it—or put him further into a state of denial.'

She already knew that, had heard as much from the doctor who had initially dealt with her father. It was for that very reason that she had taken such extreme measures, such as moving house, and her dealings with

Stephens Publishing all made through a PO box, to keep all of the publicity concerning the author J. I. Watson away from him.

'He doesn't need to see a psychiatrist,' she insisted stubbornly. 'And you had *no* right to interfere after I had expressly told you not to do so.'

'Jinx, I told you, I *didn't*— Damn it!' He finally stood up, his height and sheer physical presence immediately dominating the room. 'Do you like being mad at me? Is that it? Is that what this is really all about?' he queried shrewdly. 'Get mad at me, stay mad at me, and the attraction between us can be kept at a distance, too?'

Her eyes had widened at the accusation, the colour receding from her cheeks now as she realized the truth behind his words. It was easier to be angry with him, and to stay angry with him, than it was to fight the attraction she felt towards him. Than to accept the love she felt for him...

'Do you really believe that, Jinx?' Once again Nik was standing far too close, his warmth reaching out and touching her, his breath gently stirring the tendrils of hair at her temples.

She swallowed hard, her expression defiant as she looked up at him. 'You're changing the subject, Nik—'

'No, I don't believe I am,' he returned slowly, his eyes probing the steadiness of her gaze. 'Why do you need so desperately to push me away, Jinx?'

'There's nothing desperate about it!' she denied resentfully.

'Oh, I think that there is,' he murmured consideringly. 'Why, Jinx?'

'Why do you think?'

He shook his head. 'You tell me.'

She didn't want to tell him, didn't want to acknowledge this complete weakness she had where he was concerned. Nik Prince was a man who indulged in brief, meaningless relationships; what she wanted was a lifetime, an eternity, of a passionate, loving marriage. But that was unobtainable. Laughable when put together with Nik. She would have laughed at herself if loving him didn't hurt so much!

'We're completely different, Nik—'

'I'm a man, you're a woman; I believe it's a combination that usually works,' he taunted.

Her eyes flashed deeply blue at his levity. 'Laugh if you want to, Nik, but I—'

'I find very little to laugh at about this situation,' he assured her grimly. 'In the past I've met a woman, we've been attracted to each other, we've satisfied that attraction, and moved on. With you everything is so complicated—'

'I'm sorry,' she choked, biting hard on her bottom lip as the tears that suddenly burnt her eyes threatened to fall hotly down her cheeks. 'We could always be attracted to each other, miss out the middle bit, and just move on.'

He reached out to grasp her arms, not hurting her, but not about to release her, either. 'Can we?'

She felt like a moth mesmerized by the flame, held fascinated in the sheer intensity of that silver gaze, at the same time knowing she wanted nothing more than to lose herself in the burning pleasure of Nik's kisses, to know the hard desire of his body against hers, a desire she more than matched.

'Jinx…!' Nik groaned throatily before his head bent and his lips claimed hers, at the same time enfolding her softness against the contours of his body.

Fighting this man was impossible when she wanted him as much as he obviously wanted her. Jinx gave up any idea of even trying to do so as her lips parted beneath his to allow his marauding tongue access to the moist warmth beneath.

His hair felt like silk beneath her fingertips as they curled into his nape. She slid her body up his as she moved to return the intimacy of his kiss, gasping slightly as the sensitive tips of her breasts brushed against the hardness of his chest, feeling heavy and full in their arousal.

Staying 'mad' at him wasn't even an option at this moment!

Every inch of her felt as if it were on fire, totally alive and attuned to Nik's caresses, his hands cupping her breasts now, thumbs moving rhythmically across the hardened nipples.

Jinx gasped her pleasure, Nik at once taking advantage of her open mouth as his tongue probed even deeper, searching out every tingling nerve ending, filling her, claiming her.

She couldn't breathe—forgot to breathe!—the warmth between her thighs building to a raging fire, a fire that only grew more intense as she moved restlessly against his hardness.

Her neck arched as Nik's lips trailed across her cheek to the exposed column of her throat, sending a shiver of longing down her spine as he nibbled the lobe of her ear before continuing his exploration of the creamy hollows at the base of her throat, licking, tasting her there, before moving lower.

She had no idea who had unbuttoned her blouse, Nik or herself. She only knew that her bra was no barrier to Nik's questing lips and tongue as they moved from the swell of her breasts to capture first one roused nipple and then the other, Jinx at once feeling a rush of warm moisture between her thighs that sent her completely over the edge.

She began to unbutton his shirt, and then lost patience, simply pulling the garment apart, hearing the tearing of the silky material as a couple of the buttons actually popped off, but unheeding of it as she bared his chest to her own searching hands and lips. She reveled in the feel of the silky hair covering his tanned skin, hearing his own gasp of pleasure as her tongue teased the hardened nubs she found nestled there, at the same time as she felt the leap of his hardened shaft move suggestively against her.

One of her hands moved down the length of his chest, down over the flatness of his stomach, desperately needing to touch him, to know the joy of that pulsing flame as he—

Nik's hands moved suddenly as he cradled each of her cheeks so that he could raise her face to look intensely into her eyes. 'Be absolutely sure this is what you want, Jinx,' he groaned. 'Because I'm rapidly reaching the point of no return!'

She had passed it long ago, long before today, before yesterday, probably the first time she'd looked at him. This was the man she was destined to love, the only man she was destined to love, and she wanted him with a fierceness she hadn't known she was capable of.

She steadily held his gaze as her hand continued its downward path, touching him, caressing him, letting him know with every caress how much she wanted him.

Nik closed his eyes briefly, breathing deeply, his eyes almost black as he looked down at her once again. 'Let's go upstairs, hmm?' he prompted huskily, reaching down to take one of her hands in his as he walked towards the door. 'I very much want privacy when we make love for the first time.'

The first time…

That seemed to imply there would be other times, too. Not that it mattered; at this moment Jinx just knew she had to be with the man she loved, had to know him completely, had to give herself to him completely. Nothing less would do.

'—must be starting a cold,' Stazy murmured worriedly as she came in through the front doorway carrying baby Sam in her arms, Rik following closely behind.

Nik hastily stepped back into the sitting-room, closing the door softly behind him, silver gaze full of regret as he looked down at Jinx. 'I don't suppose it will do any good for me to ask if we can continue this at my hotel later?'

Jinx looked up at him with darkened eyes, pausing in the act of refastening her blouse to reach up and gently touch the hardness of his cheek. 'It's probably not a good idea, is it?' she murmured just as regretfully.

'I still need to talk to you,' he reminded her gruffly.

Jinx gave a rueful laugh. 'And is that what we would do if I came to your hotel later this evening—talk?' she teased. 'Somehow I don't think so.' She shook her head, finishing buttoning up her blouse. 'Some things just aren't meant to be, Nik.'

His face darkened. 'That's rubbish, and you know it!'

Did she? Seconds ago she had been prepared to take whatever Nik had to give to a relationship, no matter how little, but for some reason the fates had decided otherwise.

Nik reached out and grasped her arms. 'We make our own luck in this world, Jinx,' he rasped, as if able to read her thoughts. 'Meet me at the hotel later!' he urged forcefully.

She looked up at him, at the fierce determination in

his face, tempted, so tempted… 'I can't, Nik,' she refused breathlessly. 'My father is here. My responsibility is here,' she added more firmly.

He slowly released her, although his expression had darkened even more.

'This isn't over, Jinx,' he warned her as the murmur of voices outside could be heard approaching the sitting-room. 'Not by a long way!'

She wished that it weren't, wished that they could just go back to the way it had been a few minutes ago, aware only of each other, of pleasuring each other. But it wasn't to be. They weren't to be!

She stepped away from him, her chin raised as she bravely met his gaze. 'It's over when I say it's over, Nik,' she said, knowing by the way his mouth tightened that his desire was rapidly changing to anger.

Sometimes the only way for her to survive with this man was to make him 'mad' at her!

Nik continued to look at her for several tense seconds, once again wanting to shake her and kiss her all at the same time.

In the end he did neither, the door opening behind them to admit Stazy and Rik, his sister fussing over the baby as he grizzled in her arms. 'What is it?' Nik demanded as he took the baby from her and he instantly stopped crying.

'Just a cold, I think.' Stazy grimaced as her young son lay quietly in Nik's arms. 'But my shopping wasn't really that important.' She gave him a pointed look, the two of them knowing that she had actually 'gone shopping', and taken Rik with her, at Nik's instigation; he had said he needed to talk to Jinx on her own.

He still needed to talk to her!

Although he had definitely enjoyed what had happened between them more than he would just talking to Jinx. It was when they talked that things seemed to go wrong between them.

Which didn't for a moment change the fact that his real reason for being alone with Jinx, the conversation he needed to have with her, still remained unspoken.

'I was just trying to persuade Jinx into having dinner with me this evening,' he told Stazy, his gaze speaking volumes.

'What a lovely idea!' Stazy smiled brightly at the other woman. 'I'm sure your father will be absolutely fine with Rik and myself,' she added before Jinx could comment.

He never had underestimated his sister's intelligence, but at this moment Nik could have kissed Stazy for the way she had dismissed Jinx's reason for refusing before it even materialized.

'Absolutely fine,' Rik echoed softly, blue eyes brimming with amusement as he looked at Nik. 'What happened to your shirt?' he teased. 'You look as if you've been in a fight. Or something,' he added speculatively.

Or something…

Nik didn't so much as look at Jinx, but nevertheless he knew that her face had flushed fiery red as Rik drew attention to the fact that Nik's shirt was completely unbuttoned, that several of those buttons were actually lying on the carpet. Having fallen there when Jinx had wrenched them off earlier…

'I caught it on the door handle.' He easily held his younger brother's gaze, challenging him to take the subject any further.

'Really?' Rik smiled mockingly.

'Yes—really,' Nik insisted, silver eyes like shards of glass as he gave his brother a warning look. 'Sam seems to be okay now, Stazy.' He handed her back her sleeping son. 'It was probably having Rik along that upset him,' he taunted.

'I wondered how long that would be in coming,' his brother murmured, obviously having been well aware that he wouldn't escape retribution for the shirt remark.

'Then you weren't disappointed, were you?' Nik drawled.

Rik grinned. 'I rarely am where you're concerned.'

The two men shared a smile of mutual affection before Nik decided that Jinx had had long enough to get over her feelings of embarrassment in front of his brother and sister. 'I'll call for you at about seven-thirty, shall I?'

She gave him a frowning look. 'I don't think, after that reporter yesterday morning, that going to your hotel is a good idea.'

Nik's mouth tightened at her reference to the reporter; that was what he needed to talk to her about. And preferably before anyone else had a chance to do so. 'We won't be eating at my hotel. Besides,' he added firmly as she would have spoken, 'I've changed hotels.'

Jinx blinked. 'That was rather sudden, wasn't it?'

'But necessary,' he bit out grimly, knowing that once the press realized they were wasting their time by staking out Jinx's home they would turn their attention to his hotel. He could see by the suddenly dismayed expression on Jinx's face that she realized it too.

'I can never understand why he doesn't stay here like Rik does,' Stazy said.

'Can't you?' Rik teased.

'You could always move in here now.' Stazy ignored Rik's remark and turned to Nik. 'After all, Jinx is here, and—'

'I think we'll leave things as they are for the time

being, Stazy,' Nik interrupted before taking a light hold
of Jinx's arm. 'Walk me to the door, hmm?' he prompted
huskily.

She nodded, needing to escape from Stazy's and Rik's
knowing gazes, if only for a few minutes.

'They know, don't they?' Jinx sighed once they were
alone in the hallway.

'That you were about to rip my clothes off when they
arrived back so unexpectedly? Oh, yes, I think—'

'I wasn't!' she instantly protested, her look of apprehension turning to a rueful smile as she looked up and
found Nik smiling down at her. 'Well…okay, I was,' she
conceded awkwardly, at the same time trying to pull the
ragged edges of his shirt back together. 'I'll have to buy
you another shirt.' She winced. 'This one is beyond re-
pair.' She seemed slightly dazed that she could have been
the one responsible for that.

Nik reached up and put his hand beneath her chin,
looking down into the fragile beauty of her face. 'You
can rip as many shirts off my back as you please, Jinx,'
he assured her huskily.

'Don't!' She groaned her renewed embarrassment.

He bent his head and gently brushed his lips against
hers. 'Do,' he encouraged softly.

Her gaze suddenly avoided his. 'I—I'm afraid I'm not
as—as experienced, as the other women in your life have
probably been—' She broke off as Nik put silencing fingers against her lips.

He looked at her consideringly, that blush in her
cheeks, the slight look of bewilderment in her eyes. 'You
aren't experienced at all, are you?' he realized slightly
breathlessly, more pleased than he could ever have
guessed if that was the case.

In the past he had always been involved with women

who were experienced, deliberately so, wanting no un-
wanted complications in his life, and yet the possibility
of being Jinx's first lover—her only lover…?—somehow
exhilarated him.

Jinx's gaze didn't quite meet his. 'There never seemed
to be the time. First school. Then university. Teaching.'
She shrugged awkwardly. 'I didn't—'

'Don't apologize, Jinx,' he cut in decisively.

'I'm not apologizing,' she snapped indignantly. 'And
I'm not completely inexperienced, either. Just because I
said I wasn't as experienced as your other women doesn't
mean—'

'Don't tell me any more, Jinx.' He winced, really not
wanting to hear any of the details.

What was this woman doing to him? What had she
already done to him that he could feel such burning jeal-
ousy for faceless men who might so much as even have
kissed her?

Maybe he needed to at least have figured that out before they had dinner together this evening!

'No, you're right,' she conceded. 'We really don't
need to exchange stories about our individual sexual ex-
periences. It could take several hours to list all yours—
and if we're going to have dinner this evening, I would
like to find some time for eating!'

Nik's gaze narrowed ominously at what he guessed
was a deliberate attempt on Jinx's part to put distance
between them.

Not that he could exactly blame her; his own response
to her surprised the life out of him, so how much more
disturbing must she find her attraction towards a man
like him?

But at least she had agreed to have dinner with him this evening; it was definitely a step in the right direction.

Of what he still wasn't absolutely sure. But he did know he had no intention of letting Jinx slip out of his life...

CHAPTER FOURTEEN

JINX had no idea how she had come to be having dinner with Nik this evening. One minute she had been refusing the invitation, and the next the Prince family had seemed to have the entire thing worked out—including Stazy loaning her a dress to wear for the evening.

This dress, Jinx frowned as she looked at her reflection in the full-length mirror that adorned one wall of the bedroom she occupied in the Hunters' home. It was a simply designed dress, a black silk sheath that reached down to just above her knees—it must have been microscopically short on the much taller Stazy!—and yet Jinx knew that it carried a designer label, that its demure styling was deceptive, that the silk material clung to breasts and thighs as she moved.

But when they had hurriedly left the house earlier this morning there hadn't been time to pack more than the minimum of essentials—and a dress she could wear for a dinner date had not been included in that description.

A dinner date...

Was this really a dinner date with Nik? Of course it was. But it was because he needed to talk to her, and he couldn't do it here in front of his brother and sister.

Just keep remembering that, Jinx, she warned herself as she went downstairs to meet Nik and found him standing in the hallway looking up at her with admiring grey eyes.

Amazing. Incredible. She had fallen in love with this

man, was in love with him, and yet the two of them had never even gone out on a date together.

'You look lovely,' Nik complimented her huskily as she joined him at the bottom of the wide staircase.

'It's Stazy's dress,' Jinx instantly blurted out—and then wondered why she had done such a thing; it was certainly a good way to put an end to that particular conversation.

Although some of her flustered response, she knew, was due to her complete awareness of Nik in the black evening suit and snowy white shirt; he looked gorgeous! Lethally so…

Nik gave a rueful smile, as if he was well aware of what she was trying to do. 'Setting the tone for the evening, Jinx?' he drawled, taking a light hold of her elbow as they walked to the door.

'Sorry?'

He shrugged broad shoulders before opening the car door for her to get inside. 'If I say, "It never looked as good on Stazy", then I'm insulting my sister, and if I say nothing, then I'm insulting you.' He walked around the car and got in beside her. 'I can't win either way.'

Was that really what she had been doing? If so, she didn't think she had meant to. Her defensive instincts seemed to have kicked in automatically this time!

'Sorry.' She grimaced.

Nik chuckled. 'It's not a problem,' he assured her, putting the car in gear and driving away from the house.

She frowned. 'It isn't?'

'No.' He still smiled. 'It's a lovely evening, Jinx. I have you at my side, a table booked for the two of us at a romantic Italian restaurant I know; I have no intention of allowing you to annoy me into losing sight of that!'

When he put it like that…!

Although that wasn't the reason they were here, was it? 'I thought you said we had something we needed to talk about this evening,' she reminded him.

His mouth tightened slightly before he forced himself to relax again. 'You're dogged, Jinx, I'll give you that,' he conceded with a slight edge to his voice. 'Yes, we do have something we need to talk about, but I believe that can wait until after our meal.'

By that time she might be so under his spell that it wouldn't matter whether he talked or not—she would just want him to kiss her!

But maybe that was the plan...?

'Nik—'

'Let's just call a truce until after we've eaten, hmm?' he cut in deliberately. 'Indigestion is something to be avoided, not a prerequisite to the evening!'

He was right, Jinx knew he was right, and yet she was too aware of Nik as he sat beside her, in every way. He looked so tall and handsome, a fact borne out by the way the other women turned to look at him as they entered the restaurant together a short time later. And it was all too easy when she looked at the elegant strength of his hands to remember the way he had touched her earlier today, the caress of those hands against her bare skin. The fact that knowledge was reflected back at her in the warmth of his eyes every time he looked at her certainly wasn't helping, either!

'Let's order, shall we?' he encouraged as she would have spoken.

This was unreal. He was unreal. She would wake up tomorrow morning and realize that all of this had been a dream. A warm, wonderful dream.

Except she didn't want to wake up. Not unless it was

in this man's arms, the two of them intimately entwined in the comfort of a huge double bed, both of them naked.

'You've gone very quiet,' Nik murmured once they had given the waiter their order.

Her brows rose over steady blue eyes. 'I thought that was what you wanted.'

'Jinx, you aren't ready yet to hear what I want!' he grated frustratedly.

He might be surprised about that—because it was probably what she wanted too! Damn tomorrow. It could take care of itself. For once in her life she just wanted to forget caution, forget everything but Nik and the touch of his skin against hers.

It had been like this from that first evening, she realized slightly dazedly, a complete awareness of Nik as the man she wanted to be with, the man she wanted to make love with, the man she was in love with.

She drew in a deep breath. 'Nik, perhaps we shouldn't bother with dinner—'

'Jinx, I'm not about to let you run out on me again now!' he rasped, his hand reaching across the table to tightly clasp hers. 'Just give me a chance, hmm? You might find that you like me after all!'

Like him? She loved everything about this man, from the way he looked, the way he had come to her rescue, not once, but twice, his gentleness with her father, to the obvious close relationship he had with his sister and two brothers.

She smiled. 'Nik, you misunderstood what I was going to say. I—the thing is—' God, there had to be a better way than this, a more sophisticated way, to tell a man you wanted to go somewhere private with him and make love! Except sophistication had never been something she was good at…

'I—oh, damn!' he muttered grimly as the mobile phone in his jacket pocket began to ring. 'You aren't going anywhere,' he told Jinx before answering the call.

Jinx was very pleased not to be the person on the other end as Nik scowled into the telephone receiver. To say he was terse as he took the call would be a definite understatement, although his initial aggression calmed down as he made just yes or no answers.

Jinx was left with the dilemma of whether or not she resumed her conversation once his call was over, or simply steered it onto a safer subject.

Coward, she instantly rebuked herself.

Maybe, but wasn't she just going to be more hurt when the relationship was over if the two of them had made love? Maybe she should have thought of that earlier! Because if she knew anything at all about Nik, then he wouldn't let the subject go until he had got the truth out of her...

And the truth was that she was in love with him.

Why it had to be this man, she had no—

'Jinx.'

She looked up at the sound of her name, having been so lost in thought that she hadn't realized his telephone conversation had come to an end. But the expression on his face, compassion mixed with concern, was enough to jolt her out of that pleasant dreamworld where she had been imagining that Nik returned the love she felt for him.

'What is it?' she demanded.

'Your father,' he said economically, turning to signal to the waiter that the two of them were leaving. 'It's nothing for you to panic about,' he added hastily as she began to do exactly that, dropping her bag in her rush to leave. 'Stazy just thinks it might be a good idea for us to return home now.'

Jinx was no longer really listening, haphazardly pushing the things back into her bag that had fallen onto the floor, before standing up to walk dazedly towards the door.

Her father. What could possibly have happened? And why did Stazy think it might be 'a good idea' for them to forgo dinner and return immediately?

'Did Stazy say what's happened?' she demanded of Nik as soon as he joined her beside the car.

'Something about Sam. And your father. And—'

'Sam?' Jinx echoed. 'What on earth does Stazy's baby have to do with anything?'

'I don't know,' Nik answered, having already manoeuvred the car out into the London evening traffic. 'She was babbling, okay?' he explained as Jinx frowned at him. 'She said your father was crying—'

'*Crying?*' Jinx gasped. Her father hadn't shown any emotion other than smiling benevolence for eighteen months!

He nodded. 'Something to do with someone called Jamie. But as I don't know anyone called Jamie—Jinx?' He turned briefly and saw the way her face had paled to a ghastly grey colour. 'Jinx, do you know who this Jamie is?' he queried.

Oh, yes, she knew exactly who, and what, Jamie was.

Or had been.

She just hadn't thought that her father would ever remember him again...

By the time he turned the car into the driveway to Stazy's home Nik was so tense at Jinx's stubborn refusal to talk about Jamie that he could barely contain his emotions.

The fact that Jinx barely waited for him to park the car before getting out and running into the house didn't help his mood, but he made sure that he was only a couple of strides behind her, determined to get to the bottom of this situation.

Rik came out of the sitting-room as they hurried down the hallway. 'They're upstairs in the nursery,' he said before falling into step beside Jinx on the wide staircase. 'Sam woke up crying.' He spoke softly to Jinx. 'Your father heard him, went to investigate, and—he's okay, Jinx.' Rik put a reassuring hand on her arm.

Nik's tense frustration turned to burning anger as he saw his brother's hand on Jinx's arm, a red-hot wave of fury washing over him, almost making it impossible for him to think logically. He—

Rik glanced back at him. 'Cool it, Nik,' he said reprovingly. 'This isn't the time or the place.'

No, of course it wasn't. Jinx was the one they had to think of now. But that still didn't change the fact that Nik was filled with burning rage because it was his brother who seemed to be able to offer Jinx comfort, or that Rik seemed to know the reason why she needed that comfort.

What had he missed?

Because he had certainly missed something—he had a feeling that this man Jamie was the key to a lot more things than Jackson Nixon's returning emotions!

Nik stood in the doorway of the nursery as Jinx hurried across the room to where her father sat in the rocking-chair cradling a now-sleeping Sam, Stazy sitting on the carpeted floor at his feet.

Jackson Nixon looked up, his gaze no longer vague but filled with a pain that looked bottomless. 'He's very like Jamie was at this age, isn't he, Juliet?' He spoke gruffly before looking back down at the baby. 'So tiny. So defenceless.' He shook his head, that pain increasing in his eyes, his face lined with strain.

'Just listen, okay,' Rik said quietly at Nik's side as he made a move to go towards the ashen-faced Jinx. 'You're going to learn something,' he insisted at Nik's warning scowl.

'I hadn't noticed—but, yes, he's very like Jamie,' Jinx agreed huskily, reaching out to touch the baby's creamy cheek as she sat down on the carpet in front of the rocking-chair.

Her father closed his eyes briefly, seeming to be fighting back the tears. 'We loved you both so much, Juliet, your mother and I.'

'We both knew that, Daddy,' Jinx assured him emotionally.

'We married late, you see, and never thought that we would have a family.' Jackson continued to talk as if he hadn't heard Jinx's response. 'But first there was you. And then there was Jamie. Our two darling children.' He smiled at the memory. 'We wanted to wrap you both up in cotton wool and keep you safe for ever.' He shook his head, seeming unaware of the tears now falling hotly down his cheeks.

'We always knew how loved we were.' Jinx's hand tightened on his.

Jackson drew in a deep breath before continuing. 'It was so awful when Jamie was twelve and had his accident, when he could no longer walk, but had to sit in that wheelchair all day long; we felt as if we had somehow let him down. But when he died all those years later of pneumonia it was even worse, as if part of us had died too. Three days later your mother did die,' he choked out. 'They said she had a heart attack, but I know better.

She had spent so many years caring for Jamie, making his life as normal as possible, that when he died her heart was broken.' He shook his head, swallowing hard.

'Are you learning?' Rik murmured beside Nik.

Oh, yes, he was learning, learning what Rik had somehow already guessed. Jamie had been Jinx's brother. Jackson's son. And he had been confined to a wheelchair for years before he'd died. Like the twelve-year-old hero of *No Ordinary Boy*...

Was that where Jinx had got her idea for the book from? Was it because of her brother, a sort of memorial to him and the courage he had shown—?

'In this case two and two do make five,' Rik gently interrupted his churning thoughts.

Two and two made—?

And suddenly he knew what Rik had somehow guessed: Jamie Nixon wasn't just the hero of *No Ordinary Boy*—he had written it! Jinx's brother Jamie was the author J. I. Watson!

CHAPTER FIFTEEN

J<small>INX</small> sat in an armchair eyeing Nik warily as he stood in front of the unlit fireplace in the Hunters' elegant sitting-room, the two of them alone.

For eighteen months Jinx had prayed for this day, had willed her father to get better, knowing that it was the shock of, first Jamie's unexpected death, quickly followed by her mother's, that had put him into the cocoon-like state where nothing and no one could harm him.

Denial, the initial doctor had called it, a diagnosis backed up by Ben Travis a short time ago after he had spent an hour or so talking with her father, Jinx having finally agreed to having the other man called in.

Her father was asleep now, aided by medication from Ben Travis, the other man promising to return first thing in the morning. Although he had assured Jinx that he believed they were through the worst of it now, that her father was well on the way to a complete mental recovery.

Stazy and Rik had drifted off to their respective bedrooms once Ben Travis had left, which just left herself and the now-pacing Nik...

Only!

She had been too busy with her father for the last couple of hours to pay much attention to his reaction to what was going on, but she had known that couldn't last, that she owed him some sort of explanation. Where to start— that was the problem!

'Did Jamie write more than two books?' Nik spoke before she had the chance.

Her eyes opened in alarm as she stared up at him. 'You know…?' she gasped softly. 'Did Rik—?'

'No, my little brother kept your secret,' Nik assured her grimly, obviously far from pleased.

'He guessed.' Jinx shrugged. 'While you were out this morning the two of us talked. He's a writer too. He told me that he knew those books hadn't been written by a woman. You had told him about my family, about my mother and Jamie. He guessed the truth,' she recited flatly.

In fact, once she'd got over her initial dismay when she'd spoken to Rik earlier today, when he'd told her how he knew the truth, she had felt relieved that at last someone other than herself did.

She stood up restlessly. 'There are five books in all,' she revealed. 'I had no idea Jamie had written them until after— He left them for me in his will,' she hurried on, not wanting to dwell on the death of her beloved younger brother. 'With a request for me to send them to a publisher. He wanted to try and reach out to other people in his position, to help them, and able-bodied people, to realize that the wheelchair wasn't everything, that there were still people inside the wheelchair. The stories are a sort of legacy, I think, something he could leave behind him.'

The dilemma of her brother's request, when taken into account with their father's fragile mental health following Jamie's death quickly followed by that of her mother, had consumed her for days, weeks, before she had finally typed the first story up and sent it to James Stephens. She had simply had no idea that the book was going to be so popular, that the whole situation was going to explode in her face.

'All of the royalties from the books are to go to charities that help people like Jamie,' she added.

Nik's face softened slightly. 'Why didn't you tell me the truth?'

Jinx looked at him beneath lowered lashes. 'That I'm not the author J. I. Watson any more than my father is? That it was my dead brother who wrote them?' She shook her head. 'That wouldn't have helped me to keep the circus of the publicity away from my father.'

'But I could have helped,' he insisted. 'Damn it, Jinx!' He sighed frustratedly. 'You should have told me,' he repeated heavily.

She looked at him searchingly. 'But you were only interested in the movie rights—'

'Have I so much as mentioned them the last few days? Have I?' he demanded, grey gaze easily holding hers.

'No...' she finally conceded. 'But that doesn't mean you aren't still interested—'

'Jinx.' He reached out and grasped her arms, his fingers gentle but still immovable. 'The only thing I'm interested in is you,' he admitted. 'Just you. Forget the book. Forget the movie. Forget everything else.' His voice lowered huskily. 'Just you,' he repeated gruffly.

Jinx gazed up at him wonderingly, her gaze searching now, finding only gentleness and understanding in his expression. And something else. Something she was almost afraid to put a name to...

'I love you, Jinx.' Nik obviously felt no such fear. 'I love you, and I want to marry you. And if you think I've been determined where the movie rights to *No Ordinary Boy* are concerned, you're going to find that's been quite mild to the campaign I'm going to make on your heart!' He gave a self-derisive smile. 'I'm just going to hang around and make a nuisance of myself until you can't do anything else but fall in love with me!'

Jinx felt as if she had been in shock since the moment Nik had first said he loved her, but at this last statement she couldn't help but smile, albeit a tearfully happy smile. 'More of a nuisance than you've already been?' she asked shakily.

'Oh, much more,' he assured her.

She smiled through her tears. 'Then it's just as well I'm already in love with you, isn't it?' she teased.

'You're already—!' For once in their acquaintance Nik looked stunned. Although that didn't last long as he began to smile, love lighting up his eyes now as he took in the full import of what she was saying.

Jinx nodded shyly. 'Why do you think, in the restaurant earlier, I was about to suggest that I would like to leave so that we could go somewhere private and make love?'

His eyes widened. 'That's what you were about to say?'

'Oh, yes,' she breathed softly, moving into the warmth of his arms, her face raised invitingly to his. 'I love you very much, Nikolas Prince. And I would love nothing more than to be your wife,' she told him seconds before his head lowered and his mouth claimed hers in a kiss so filled with love it made her heart ache with happiness.

Heaven. Nik was her own piece of heaven. The man she had been searching for all her life. Her Prince.

* * *

How he loved this woman! She was the other half of him. The 'something' that had been missing all of his adult life. She was the love of his life!

All of which he had realized earlier today when he'd sat down to analyze what it was he felt towards her. Analyze! Love wasn't something that could be analyzed. It just was. And he loved Jinx more than life itself, knew that he could only be complete with her at his side, as his beloved wife.

'Mmm,' she murmured happily some time later as he reluctantly released her lips, smiling up at him with such love he felt as if he were going to burst with the emotion. 'Do you think Stazy and Rik would notice if you were to stay the night in my bedroom?'

'They might not, but I would—and I have no intention of us sharing a bedroom until you are officially my wife,' Nik told her firmly, at the same time wondering at himself for these newly realized protective feelings.

He wanted everything to be right for Jinx, everything done exactly as it should be, wanted her to wear a white gown as she came down the aisle to him, wanted their wedding night to be the first they shared together.

Damn it, against all the odds, since meeting Jinx he had discovered he was just an old-fashioned romantic, after all!

Jinx chuckled softly as she correctly read the slightly dazed expression on his face. 'Bet you can't believe you said that, can you?' she teased lovingly.

'No,' he admitted wryly. 'But I do mean it, Jinx. It will just have to be the most rapidly arranged wedding in history!' He groaned as her soft curves nestled lovingly against his.

'It will be.'

Nik put Jinx determinedly away from him as he could feel his emotions—and his body!—rapidly spiralling out of control. Although he couldn't release her completely, needing to touch her, to know that she was there, that she was his. He twined his fingers with hers as the two of them sat down on the sofa, Jinx's head resting against his shoulder, his lips against the silky softness of her hair.

He still couldn't believe this was happening, had felt sure that Jinx must hate him after the way he had hounded her over the movie rights of *No Ordinary Boy*, had resigned himself earlier to winning her love, to showing her that he wasn't the man the press said he was, deciding that he would have to embark on an old-fashioned courtship. Not that he was completely aware of exactly what that was, he just knew that Jinx deserved to be wooed, that he would win her love, no matter how long it took.

He still found the fact that she was already in love with him completely overwhelming.

But he would be grateful that she did until the day he died…

'You were going to tell me something at the restaurant earlier,' she reminded him drowsily.

He had forgotten all about that the last half an hour or so! Not surprising really, with Jinx lying so warm, soft, and loving in his arms. But it was one last explanation that she probably deserved.

Even if he did come out of it in a less than positive light, he allowed with an inward grimace of apprehension.

'Nik?' Jinx sat up to prompt concernedly.

He reached up to cradle each side of her face with his hands as he looked at her. 'Jinx, I haven't always been— fair, shall we say, in my dealings with women—'

'I thought we had agreed on not having those sort of confessions,' she teased.

'We have.' He nodded. 'Except that one of the women I was briefly—involved with, was Jane Morrow.' He looked at her anxiously, half fearing Jinx's reaction to his confession, and yet knowing he had to make it.

'My editor? *That* Jane Morrow…?' Jinx said slowly, a frown now appearing between her glorious violet-blue eyes.

'Yes.' Nik swallowed hard. 'It wasn't anything serious, a couple of dinners, a few kisses.' He grimaced in self-disgust. 'But my motives weren't exactly honourable.' Anything but, he could now acknowledge with distaste, knowing that loving Jinx had changed him in ways he could never have imagined, that he never wanted to do anything that would hurt, upset, or disappoint her. And his brief relationship with Jane Morrow, the reasons behind it, were guaranteed to do all three of those things.

He watched Jinx anxiously, her eyes narrowed, her thoughts all inwards. If he should lose her now—!

Finally she nodded. 'Jane Morrow was the one who told the press about me, wasn't she?' she realized astutely. 'That's why that reporter was at the hotel following you, hoping you would lead them to me. Why they were able to follow me from the publishing house yesterday. She telephoned them before coming to James Stephens's office and told them the author J. I. Watson was there, didn't she?'

'She did,' he confirmed heavily; as long as the two of

them continued talking, perhaps it would all come out right after all.

'But why?' Jinx frowned. 'I'd never done anything to her—'

'No, but I had,' Nik put in flatly. 'I used my friendship with her to find you. And once I had, I—well, let's say that Jane had good reason not to feel particularly friendly towards me.'

'She wanted to get back at you,' Jinx realized. 'She was trying to hurt you, wasn't she?' She shook her head. 'Jane Morrow believed that if she made it look like you were responsible for bringing publicity to J. I. Watson, someone who had made it perfectly plain he didn't want any, then he would categorically refuse to let you have the film rights to *No Ordinary Boy*. That's it, isn't it, Nik?'

He nodded. 'Earlier this morning I managed to locate the reporter from the hotel. She didn't want to talk to me at first, but while discussing the large sum of money that had been paid to her source for supplying information on J. I. Watson she inadvertently revealed who that source was.'

'But I thought reporters didn't reveal their sources?' Jinx frowned.

'They don't usually. This one wouldn't have done, either, but once she mentioned that her source was a senior member of Stephens Publishing staff, and as such entirely reliable, it didn't take too much intelligence to guess that it was Jane Morrow. Besides, the reporter didn't exactly luck out; she wasn't averse to extracting a price herself for having given me the information.'

'What sort of price?' Jinx's eyes were wide.

'An in-depth interview with Zak,' he revealed with satisfaction. 'Not that he knows about it yet...!' And his little brother was going to be far from pleased when he did know, but at the time of asking Nik hadn't hesitated in giving the reporter exactly what she wanted. Besides, the reporter was quite attractive; Zak might just enjoy the experience. Although Nik wouldn't count on it! 'But that isn't important at the moment.' He dismissed the argument he knew he was going to have with Zak, sitting up to look anxiously at Jinx. 'The thing is that, although Jane Morrow may have made those telephone calls, and accepted that money for doing so, I'm really the one responsible for bringing the press down on you. If I hadn't—' He broke off, Jinx's fingers pressing lightly against his lips.

Jinx shook her head. 'We hadn't even met when you were involved with Jane Morrow.'

'But I was only involved with her as a way of getting to you—'

'Nik, she's a grown woman in her thirties, hardly a child that you seduced and then abandoned!' Jinx reasoned. 'Okay, so your behaviour was—less than honourable, and I'm sorry that it happened, but your behaviour is no excuse for hers. What she did was totally vindictive. She's my editor, for goodness' sake—'

'Was,' Nik put in softly. 'Once James Stephens became aware of what had happened, he dismissed her.'

Jinx shrugged. 'I could never have worked with her again anyway after she had betrayed my trust in that way.'

Nik swallowed hard. 'You aren't going to change your mind about marrying me?' He felt as if he had the sword of Damocles hanging over his head as he waited for her answer.

'Oh, no,' she reassured him without hesitation, moving to kiss him lingeringly on the lips. 'Although I am going to make sure that nothing like Jane Morrow ever happens again,' she added warningly.

Nik's arms tightened around her possessively as he began to breathe again. 'You won't need to,' he assured her with certainty. 'I love you, Jinx Nixon. Only you. For always.'

'Mmm, I like the sound of that,' she murmured, her lips only centimetres away from his.

So did he, he decided as his lips claimed hers in a kiss that left neither of them in any doubt that what they had between them was for ever.

EPILOGUE

'Do YOU think the two of us can leave any time soon?'

Jinx turned to smile warmly at her husband. Her husband of only six hours. Her husband Nik. Her husband Nik Prince.

She had sat in the hairdressers' this morning as her hair had been styled and curled, tiny white rosebuds amongst the curls in place of a veil, and practised saying that phrase, 'My husband, Nik'. Daydreaming, really, and yet the whole of the last three weeks had passed as if a wonderful dream.

First had come telling their families of their intention to marry. Then had come the arrangements for the wedding, something Nik had managed to sort out with ease. Then had come the family statement to the press concerning the real identity of the author J. I. Watson, a statement that had been met with only warmth and understanding. In fact, if anything it had renewed the sales of *No Ordinary Boy*, while at the same time creating a clamouring for the second book to be published.

Her father still found the attention afforded to his dead son a little overwhelming on occasions, but as each day passed, with gentle guidance from Ben Travis, he was getting stronger, his pride in his son helping with that recovery.

If Jinx could have known this would be the result of explaining exactly who the author J. I. Watson really was, then she would have done it much sooner!

'Very soon,' she answered Nik, leaning into his body,

the warmth of her gaze telling him exactly how much she longed for them to be alone, too. 'Hasn't it been a beautiful day?' she murmured dreamily as she glanced around at all the happily smiling wedding guests.

In fact, the wedding list that Nik had drawn up for his side of the family read like a 'who's who' in the world of celebrities, a fact that held her more staid family and friends in thrall.

'Why is Zak scowling like that?' Jinx frowned as she noticed her new brother-in-law's less-than-happy demeanour.

Nik was grinning with satisfaction as she turned to look up at him enquiringly.

Her eyes widened. 'You didn't choose today of all days to tell him about that in-depth interview you promised on his behalf?' she guessed, knowing he had been putting off the dreaded moment.

Nik's grin widened as he nodded. 'I didn't think even he would hit me on my wedding day! Besides, he won't stay too mad at me once he knows you've requested that he take the part of the father when we make the movie of No Ordinary Boy.'

Jinx began to smile herself, that smile turning to a chuckle as her arms slid up her husband's chest to link her hands at his nape. 'I'm ready to leave if you are,' she told him throatily.

'More than ready,' he murmured with promise. 'In fact, if I don't make love to you soon, Mrs Prince, I may just go quietly insane!'

One of her hands moved to caress the hardness of his cheek. 'And we can't have that, can we?'

'Not for another forty or fifty years at least!' he agreed huskily.

Forty or fifty years. A lifetime. For ever.

With Nik.

MILLS & BOON

Live the emotion

Modern
romance™

THE DISOBEDIENT VIRGIN by Sandra Marton

Catarina Mendes has been dictated to all her life. Now, with her twenty-first birthday, comes freedom – but it's freedom at a price. Jake Ramirez has become her guardian. He must find a man for her to marry. But Jake is so overwhelmed by her beauty that he is tempted to keep Cat for himself...

A SCANDALOUS MARRIAGE by Miranda Lee

Sydney entrepreneur Mike Stone has a month to get married – or he'll lose a business deal worth billions. Natalie Fairlane, owner of the *Wives Wanted* introduction agency, is appalled by his proposition! But the exorbitant fee Mike is offering for a temporary wife is *very* tempting…!

SLEEPING WITH A STRANGER by Anne Mather

Helen Shaw's holiday on the island of Santos should be relaxing. But then she sees Greek tycoon Milos Stephanides. Years ago they had an affair – until, discovering he was untruthful, Helen left him. Now she has something to hide from Milos…

AT THE ITALIAN'S COMMAND by Cathy Williams

Millionaire businessman Rafael Loro is used to beautiful women who agree to his every whim – until he employs dowdy but determined Sophie Frey! Sophie drives him crazy! But once he succeeds in bedding her, his thoughts of seduction turn into a need to possess her…

On sale 4th November 2005

Available at most branches of WHSmith, Tesco, ASDA, Borders, Eason, Sainsbury's and most bookshops

Visit www.millsandboon.co.uk

MILLS & BOON
Live the emotion

1005/01b

Modern
romance™

PRINCE'S PLEASURE by *Carole Mortimer*

Reporter Tyler Harwood is ecstatic when she gets the
chance to interview handsome Hollywood actor Zak
Prince. Zak finds working with this stunning brunette fun!
But someone is out to make mischief from their growing
closeness – and soon candid pictures appear in the press…

HIS ONE-NIGHT MISTRESS by *Sandra Field*

Lia knew that billionaire businessman Seth could destroy
her glittering career. But he was so attractive that she
succumbed to him – for one night! Eight years on, when
he sees Lia in the papers, Seth finds that he has a love-
child, and is determined to get her back!

THE ROYAL BABY BARGAIN by *Robyn Donald*

Prince Caelan Bagaton has found the woman who
kidnapped his nephew and now he is going to exact his
revenge… For Abby Metcalfe, the only way to continue
taking care of the child is to agree to Caelan's demands
– and that means marriage!

BACK IN HER HUSBAND'S BED by *Melanie Milburne*

Seeing Xavier Knightly, the man she divorced five years
ago, changes Carli Gresham's life. Their marriage may be
dead, but their desire is alive – and three months later
Carli tells Xavier a shocking secret! But by wanting her to
love him again Xavier faces the biggest battle of his life…

Don't miss out!
On sale 4th November 2005

Available at most branches of WHSmith, Tesco, ASDA,
Borders, Eason, Sainsbury's and most bookshops

Visit www.millsandboon.co.uk

researching the cure

The facts you need to know:

- **One woman in nine** in the United Kingdom will develop breast cancer during her lifetime.

- Each year **40,700** women are newly diagnosed with breast cancer and around **12,800** women will die from the disease. However, survival rates are improving, with on average 77 per cent of women still alive five years later.

- **Men can also suffer from breast cancer**, although currently they make up less than one per cent of all new cases of the disease.

Britain has one of the highest breast cancer death rates in the world. Breast Cancer Campaign wants to understand why and do something about it. Statistics cannot begin to describe the impact that breast cancer has on the lives of those women who are affected by it and on their families and friends.

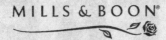

4 FREE

BOOKS AND A SURPRISE GIFT!

We would like to take this opportunity to thank you for reading this Mills & Boon® book by offering you the chance to take FOUR more specially selected titles from the Modern Romance™ series absolutely FREE! We're also making this offer to introduce you to the benefits of the Reader Service™—

- ★ FREE home delivery
- ★ FREE gifts and competitions
- ★ FREE monthly Newsletter
- ★ Exclusive Reader Service offers
- ★ Books available before they're in the shops

Accepting these FREE books and gift places you under no obligation to buy, you may cancel at any time, even after receiving your free shipment. Simply complete your details below and return the entire page to the address below. You don't even need a stamp!

YES! Please send me 4 free Modern Romance books and a surprise gift. I understand that unless you hear from me, I will receive 6 superb new titles every month for just £2.75 each, postage and packing free. I am under no obligation to purchase any books and may cancel my subscription at any time. The free books and gift will be mine to keep in any case.

P5ZED

Ms/Mrs/Miss/Mr ....Initials ....
BLOCK CAPITALS PLEASE

Surname ....

Address ....

....

....Postcode.............................

Send this whole page to:
UK: FREEPOST CN81, Croydon, CR9 3WZ